MW00778362

LOVE

TIME ROGUES SERIES BOOK 1

MARILYN Vix

SHADOWCAT PUBLISHING
SAN JOSE, CALIFORNIA

Shadowcat Publishing

San Jose, California

This book is intended for readers eighteen and over. Adult content is meant for entertainment purposes. This book is a work of fiction. All the character names, places, or incidents are fictional. Similarities to real people, places, or events are coincidental. The author acknowledges the trademark status and trademark owners of products that are mentioned in this work of fiction.

EVERYTHING FOR LOVE

ISBN: 978-0997817027

Author: Marilyn Vix

Cover Design: James at GoOnWrite.com

Editor: Shelley Holloway,

Copy Editor: Robin J. Samuels, Shadowcat Editing

Formatting: Write Dream Repeat Book Design

Beta readers: Alain Gomez

Contents

One....................................7

Two....................................17

Three................................27

Four...................................35

Five....................................49

Six.....................................59

Seven................................69

Eight..................................81

Nine...................................93

Ten.....................................105

Eleven...............................115

Twelve...............................133

Thirteen.............................143

Fourteen............................159

Fifteen...............................171

Sixteen..............................185

Seventeen.........................209

Eighteen............................225

Nineteen............................237

About the Author...............257

Acknowledgments.............258

More by Marilyn Vix..........261

Dedicated to Anne Rice and Carrie Fisher.
Two writers I strive to become every day.

One

Deidre climbed the stairs to his loft and rang the bell. The door slid open. Inside, he was waiting.

Strong, young, and handsome, he had brown hair that flowed down to his shoulders. She loved to flip his curls in her fingers. His tan coat was covered with flecks of paint, but was set off with a large, dark blue cravat. He always let his work spoil his clothes. It was his charm. He glowed with a smile when he met her eyes.

"Deidre, my love. What brings you to Montmartre today?"

"You," she answered as she walked through the doorway, pushing him back toward the bed.

"You are my little vixen," he said as he removed his cravat with a flick of his wrist.

"Do me a favor? Hurry."

He grabbed her around the waist, but held up a hand to stall their descent onto the bed. An expert at releasing a woman from frivolous garments, he expertly undid each of her many pearl buttons, slowly, teasing her, as her silk dress began to fall free.

One tantalizing kiss followed another as he progressed down her until the dress fell to the floor with a chorus of burgundy silk ruffles. After an admiring gaze, he swung her onto the bed.

She turned to see Philippe looking at her, his eyes focused on her bosoms as they peeked out from the top of the tight corset, swelling with each breath she took. Though she wanted to be free from its confines, she enjoyed teasing him with anticipation. She rolled onto her side, her hair starting to unravel from its pins, watching his reaction as he watched her. She smiled as he descended upon her. "What are you looking at?"

"Something I would love to paint."

He lowered himself down and kissed her gently with firm lips.

She reached for his jaw line, caressing it. Moving his hand down her leg, he slipped his fingers into the top of one stocking and then the other, slowly rolling them down her legs, kissing the insides of her warm thighs as he went. She reached down and pulled on his hair, encouraging him to return. As he rose, he began to unlace her corset, freeing her breasts, exposing her pert nipples. She caressed the front of his chest, feeling the definition, the flatness of his belly. She stopped at his waist, looking up with a smile.

"Should I continue?" she whispered.

He answered by undoing the buttons to his trousers. He sat up, allowing her to take in the gorgeous view of his body. She smiled, forgetting the past pains. She loved this time period, and Paris. It was the one thing about her job she loved. Charging her time bracelet. Sex was the main power resource for her to jump in time.

She sat up like a cat, matching his stance. They came together in another kiss, this time her exposed breasts pressed up against his naked chest. They wrapped their arms about each other, forming one being. Slowly, they lay down interwoven as legs came together.

"Just one more thing." Philippe reached down and pulled her bloomers. She felt the cold exposure that meant that she was free. He rolled back on top of her and she felt his hand as it reached for the warmth that would lead him toward her moist lips. Gently, his fingers teased her folds, making her ready. She squirmed at his caress and felt the nudges of his shaft exploring between her legs. She opened wider, anticipating the moment he would take her.

She arched her back and met him with an eager thrust. She felt the glorious eruption of power as he thrust into her. She angled herself to take him deep. She loved the feel of a man taking her. Again and again, they came together until the final explosion that released them both. It had been so long. Not since her last jump had she felt locked so closely with a man. She wrapped her arms about him, pulling him toward her, savoring the smell of the paint. She wanted to remember him like this.

She let him hold her until she came to her senses. He had a tendency to make her forget her mission. But then, often when she needed to refuel the energy capsule for the time vehicle, this happened. She forgot herself. She looked at the silver band on her right wrist. Disguised as jewelry, the glow of the center jewel let her know she'd almost charged it completely.

One more conquest, and she'd have it charged enough to travel to her next assignment. Three times were needed for each jump. She'd made a lot of contacts on this jump. A sculptor and a painter had been her research subjects. Now, she was going to have to leave 1899. Say good-bye to the lights of Paris. She sighed. Oh, she was going to miss Philippe. She enjoyed the feel of his arms around her.

She felt safe being held like this, but she knew she couldn't stay. So much had been sacrificed for this trip. If it hadn't been for James. She stopped her thoughts. She didn't want to think of her partner's ill-timed jump. He urged her to run and jump without him. The flash of the knife plunging into him. The yell from him to keep going as she dove into their time vehicle and gave the command to move into jump mode. She shook her head, trying not to shiver. No matter how much she tried to shake it off, the scene came back to her.

Philippe must have felt her movement and whispered to her, "What is it, ma chèrie?" He put his hand on her bare shoulder as she sat up.

"Nothing. Just feeling a chill now." She slowly rolled out of bed and walked over to the pillows and blankets that made up the posing area for Philippe's subjects. Reaching down, she pulled one around her and sat down on the cushions.

With her leg up and breasts free, she lay the length of the cushions on her back. Her hair fanned out around her, she looked up at the ceiling. The paint peeled in curls, making her want to pluck them. She heard footsteps and turned onto her side. "Is this how you want me?" She flipped her hair. "You've put me in the mood to pose." She needed to continue with the mission. For James.

She heard a gasp as she looked up. Philippe had regained his trousers and was looking at her, grabbing a brush. He pulled a stool and easel near him and whispered, "Don't move. I want to capture the moment."

"Really, Philippe? I could fall asleep like this." She felt relaxed and sedated as she did whenever she charged her bracelet. Researching the time of the Bohemian artists had its advantages. They lived the lives they painted and tried to capture. She'd been posing for Philippe for a month now. Her time with him was almost over.

"Could you turn your head a little this way, ma chèrie. To the left." He concentrated, now gazing at her, his lips pursed in concentration. His hair fell across his eyes, obstructing his view of his subject, as he quickly tucked it behind his ear. "Good. Hold that if you would. Oh, but don't close your eyes."

"I can't help it. You relaxed me quite a bit." She smiled as he raised one eyebrow at her.

"Remember, I need you to hold the pose. That kind of look could get me started again."

"I'm hoping so." One more entanglement with Philippe would help fill the time energy bracelet. She had to follow the schedule and jump in two days. But she needed to let him recharge. She smiled at the thought of another go with him.

"Now, don't move. Back to your original look, ma chèrie." She stopped smiling. "A little down now. Good. Yes. Keep your eyes big like that." He sighed once as he gazed back at her and went back to sketching.

"Will I have to hold this for long? It's hard looking at you like that, Philippe. So full of concentration with no shirt on." She pouted.

"Give me time. It will be worth it." He winked at her.

She gave a *humph*, blowing shiny blonde curls out of her blue eyes. "You're trying my patience, mon cher." She froze her position so Philippe could work his magic. She watched his brush strokes as much as she could. After some time of studying his technique, her eyes wandered down his torso, and she gave another *humph*. She knew the recording implant was capturing everything in this time period and the ones she'd visited in the past. Each new jump held a new artist on whom she focused, and captured movements lost to the digital age. Her job—to research the past for art techniques and if possible, get close enough to her subjects to record them—brought her close to observe like this. It was easier if she could pose for them.

"Stay still, ma chèrie. I'm getting near a stopping point."

"I hope so. I'm getting awfully lonely over here all alone." If she had to sit awhile, at least she could think of her next move. Studying the artists of the Bohemian movement had not been easy. They were a very hard group to infiltrate unless you had connections.

Luckily, she'd been supplied with a letter of introduction from a rich family needing portraits and statues for an estate. That had been her way into the circle of Bohemians. Her whole identity was made up to not interfere with history. With a lot of gold exchanged for money, she had found her way into this tight-knit group of artists. She had learned that many things could be bought. The Manual of Time Transportation Art Research pointed out that money always opened doors to finding facts in the past. She took the advice to heart and always took the role of an heiress or rich widow as her undercover identity.

She again tried to focus on the way that Philippe moved the brush on the canvas. Such use of physical paint had been unheard of for over two hundred years. To see it demonstrated by someone firsthand was amazing. No one painted by hand in her time. As he worked, smiles and sighs continued to be thrown her direction.

She had just started to nod off when she heard a triumphant, "Eh, c'est fini." Her implant must have not translated the last sentence since she was falling unconscious. As she awoke, Philippe continued in English. "You may move now, my beauty. This has been a pleasant way to spend the afternoon."

Deidre got up and stretched, feeling the pull of her body toward Philippe. She went straight for his lap and wrapped her arms around his shoulders, catching the smell of light sweat and wine that permeated his body. This was going to be the smell she associated with Montmartre. These things never made it into the research, but they were important details to remember of the experience.

"I know where we can go for dinner." She noticed the sun starting to lower through the dirt-stained windows. "There is a little café not too far from my apartment. I would love to show you. The wine and food are beyond this world. Plus, I know the owner. He owes me a few favors. I want us to eat well tonight. I might have to be leaving soon for London."

At those last words, Philippe stopped nuzzling her neck. "No, how could you say this? Why would you leave Paris?" He held her closer, but she pushed him back so she could look into his eyes. Oh, those deep brown eyes.

"It's business, Philippe. I told you I had clients that needed me in other cities. I will have to leave for London soon, but I wanted to say good-bye in the most memorable way first." She kissed him, hoping to remove the disappointment from his face. The shock of her news must be hitting him hard. He did not kiss back.

"What is wrong?"

"I am sorry. But this hurts me greatly. Please." He motioned her to get up. She stood and watched him get up and walk toward the window.

She had to tell him now. There had been ramifications to studied subjects when timeanauts just disappeared in past jumps. So, the Time Council had mandated that all subjects studied must be told prior to a timeanaut's pending departure. It wasn't good to leave a hole in history. All timeanauts followed a strict code to keep the timeline intact. She was instructed to tell everyone with whom she had contact that she was leaving for business elsewhere.

She moved toward Philippe. "I'm truly sorry, Philippe. It is something that has come up that I can't avoid." She wondered if he could hear the unease in her voice.

She had met Philippe at the start of her time in Paris, and she had known it would come to this. Being without her timeanaut partner had put her in a difficult position. She had to power her bracelet somehow. James had been a means to power her bracelet, and was her travel companion. But now that he was gone, she had no choice. And Philippe had been so attractive.

It was also difficult to understand the level of emotion that people attached to sex during this time period. She had pegged Philippe as being one of the more sensitive ones, too. Her missions often put her in the middle of the artistic interaction as a subject. With Philippe, she was lucky. Given his emotional attachment, he was giving her even greater insights into how artistic interactions created art.

She reached toward him, and he batted her hand away.

"Is it another?" He turned with a flash of rage. It was like a shadow had taken over him.

"No, Philippe, it is really another assignment, for a client. I must go research, and the only items that I can study are in London." In the year 1914, but she didn't share that out loud. This was the hardest part. Everyone always wanted an explanation. Her next jump was to the Vorticist movement in Britain.

The truth was not believable, and strictly not allowed. Those who dared to admit that they came from the future often got locked up in prison or asylums. It would interfere with the research since time was limited, always. The fact that she traveled through time to experience history and report her findings was something she could never share. Her occupation of art researcher timeanaut had no meaning here. They wouldn't exist for another 250 years. She bit her lip, knowing she had to hold back the truth.

"Go," he said quietly.

"But," she said with a hope flaming within her. It just couldn't end this way.

"No, please, my dear, go. If we must break with seeing each other, I would like it to be quick. Good travels, my love."

He turned to go to her, his eyes starting to well up. "Here." He grabbed her dress from the floor near the pallet. She began to dress as he retrieved her shoes and pantaloons. "Go with my love. I will remember you for all you have given me." He kissed her on the nose, a subtle press. Then, he traced his lips along her cheek. She stopped dressing for a moment, enjoying the caress. She closed her eyes as he continued to nuzzle her neck and then grabbed her in an embrace.

ill always remember you this way." They held each other, and then he broke away from her. After buttoning her dress, she sat down on the stool to redo the buttons of her shoes, and then stood to face him one last time.

"Continue with your art, Philippe. It is magnificent." She tried to look again into those brown eyes. "I do regret saying good-bye. But I must."

She gently reached out and cupped his cheek, then let her hand fall along his neck, caressing his shoulder, down his arm, and finally grasping his hand. He pulled it to his lips, pressing hard at the back, turning it over for one last kiss. Then, he held it to his heart. He still did not look at her. "Go in peace, my love. I will continue my art, in our love's memory. My memory of you will be my muse."

There was a moment of silence as he gave her one last, longing look. Knowing it would be easier if she left now, she turned and did not look back.

Once outside, she checked her wrist for the time charge. She did need to visit someone else before it would be full. Things were simpler when she could charge her bracelet with James. Once again, she tried to hold back the sense of loss that threatened to break through. She shook her head as she began her descent down the stairs. He was dead. She needed to carry on her mission without him. She breathed a cleansing sigh.

Maybe the sculptor would be up for an early dinner.

Two

"*Mademoiselle Douverte*, it is so good to see you." Gaston the sculptor kissed each of her cheeks before they took their seats at the small café table. "What do we have to talk about tonight?"

Deidre took a deep breath. Philippe hadn't taken the news so well. She was going to try to do better with Gaston. "I am afraid that I will have to leave Paris to return to London soon. It is some of my late husband's business that must be attended to."

Gaston nodded down toward his glass. Deidre didn't want to be responsible for the disappointment that dimmed those brilliant blue eyes. She wanted his sparkle to return. He looked up at her with a smile of mirth. Blond hair fell across his eyes. Sometimes, that look stopped her breath. "But that does leave us a bit of time to explore the possibilities of your sculpture. How many days do I have to finish my explorations of your form?"

She laughed at that. Why were the artists in Montmartre so forward all the time? "Perhaps later tonight, dear Gaston. I do so enjoy your explorations in form." She smiled back as he met her gaze. His eyes lit up with the fire of an imp.

"Then more wine may be needed. It gives you just the right amount of color to your lips and cheeks. I need to get the spacing on them just right to finish the cherub form I've based on you." He reached forward to caress her cheek. She closed her eyes as he traced her cheekbone to her lips. She pressed her lips to the tips of his fingers, and they joined in a laugh together.

Deidre took a sip of her wine and looked about the café to see who was part of the scene tonight. There were ladies of means sitting among several artists; many she had met were her friends' patrons. She noticed another artist she had been researching earlier in the month, Bertram Cleautrope. He had promise as a writer. The heated voices of two men arguing over the ideals of painting with light versus dark reached her ears from the corner of the room. As she turned her head, she noticed another watching her closely. His dark features, as well as his dark clothing, hid him in the shadows of the darkened corner. His eyes bored into her. She was startled by a voice speaking her name.

"Deidre? Is it you?" It was her friend Henri de Toulouse-Lautrec. It was by his introductions that she had been welcomed into the artistic world of Montmartre. He tipped his hat as she noticed his beard was a little longer than when she'd seen him last. He may have been too busy to clip it recently. He leaned heavily on his cane, always in hand because of a childhood riding accident that left his legs severely deformed.

Maybe it was his affliction, maybe not, but she felt an affinity for him, more so than most of the artists here. He overcame so much to become a painter and lithographic artist. She felt sad she would be leaving him soon. She knew he had only a few years before his early death. It would be such a blow to the art world surrounding him.

"Dear Henri, it is good to see you." She held out her hand and he took it, kissing it gently upon the knuckles. "And I was hoping to see you before leaving for London."

"Leaving?" Even Henri sounded startled. She was touched. "How could you leave us, precious flower, our blossoming student of all that we hold dear. We've been trying to educate you in the ways of love and truth. Why leave now?"

She smiled at his play in words. The arguments were a way to feed the minds of La Bohème. Engaging in the debates was a part of regular party talk. She picked up her wine glass. "But, monsieur, I've been well schooled. I think my education will have to come to a recess. I must travel on to continue it elsewhere." She drank to that as Gaston raised his glass to her.

She gestured to Henri. "Join us. We will drink and eat to my better understanding of love and truth. It is the reason to live and let live."

Henri smiled and tipped his head toward her. "Let us celebrate your education. To life, freedom, and love."

"The most important of all, to love," finished Gaston.

"And to you, Deidre." They both raised their glasses in another toast. "May you find the truth within what you love to do."

Deidre answered the call to finish the toast. "To our health. May we die knowing that life is too short. Find what you must do now or die trying." All three joined her in another toast as more delicacies were brought at Henri's insistence.

His family had means, and he was actually successfully making his way as an artist. In fact, he was technically a count.

In the end, all his friends were grateful and well fed when he was around. He shared his good fortune. The start of another famous Henri Lautrec party had begun.

The wine flowed. The food was consumed. Time seemed endless as the debate and conversations continued. A woman joined them, sitting closest to Henri. Deidre noticed the woman look her up and down and then overtly ignored her as she tried to get Henri's attention. But he seemed to ignore her efforts, only to listen to Deidre.

Deidre glanced over at the mysterious man in the corner. He still watched her. She knew if she stayed with friends, nothing too gruesome could happen. Luckily, she was an art researcher. She had learned silent observation and not getting too involved was best, especially for a woman on her own, even as a widow. Stick with at least one historical figure, but never get too involved.

Conversations buzzed around the table of things great and forgotten, and Deidre started to lose track. She had been gathering as much information as she could on the artists of this movement, but there were times when the research overwhelmed her. As she enjoyed what was likely to be her last taste of French cuisine for some time, she listened to the debate between Gaston and Henri on whether the true art form was sculpture or paint. Wisely, she avoided the absinthe that was brought to the table. Wine was enough to dull her edge, but she would be unable to follow the conversations if she drank the Green Fairy.

"The form cannot be surpassed by mere color. It is the essence of expression, showing the human body in its glory. Nothing could be considered greater."

"Non, non, non, Gaston." Henri's arm waved his glass of absinthe to emphasize his point. "Paint is the old medium. If we can illustrate with color and show things with the transformation of lithographs, it will revolutionize the way the world is seen." His other arm came up to point at Gaston. "The emotion of the art is what counts, not the form."

"Nonsense, Henri. You have drunk too much of the Green Fairy." He waved his hand at Henri. "She is talking to you in riddles and not letting you see reason." He took a swig from his glass, emptying it, and stacked it with the rest that littered the table. "Oh dear." He swayed at the table. "I do worry if I do not start home now, I will not make it for fear of falling. I do not want to litter the streets of Paris any more than they already are."

The table erupted with laughter as Gaston bent to take Deidre's hand. "Perhaps tomorrow, chèrie, we will finish the nymph you have inspired."

"Good night, Gaston. I will see you in the afternoon. I know that morning will likely not be an option after tonight." Again, laughter erupted from the table as Gaston stood, tipped his hat, and left in a staggering movement toward the front door.

Henri turned to Deidre, having noticed that his lady friend was disposed to talk to the more handsome writer next to their table. The café had attracted a lot of the regulars of the Bohemian scene. It was quite busy with the business of pursuing the discussions of creation, accented by the absinthe fueling the creative movement.

"Deidre dear, you and I are quite the same in many ways." Henri smiled with a sparkle in his eye. He would be the highlight in her final report on the period. He was a gentleman among poverty-stricken artists. His genuine love for the people he met made him stand out.

The wine was affecting Deidre in more ways than she antici-
pated, and focusing was becoming an issue, but she reached for
her friend's hand and asked, "Dear Henri, how are we alike?"

"We love our artists maybe far too much than what is good
for us," he said, his voice full of raw emotion.

Squeezing his hand, she said, "My dear Henri, who has hurt
you that you suffer so? Has the Green Fairy reached your heart?"

"I'm afraid so. I know that you love many of my artistic
friends, and I know it is something that a woman must decide
for herself. But I think a greater understanding of that woman
is the real truth to finding the art within her."

Deidre tried to focus on the most important bit of research
she had found yet. Henri Toulouse-Lautrec was telling her inner
secrets that only a time transportation art researcher could find
out. She needed to pay close attention to what he was going to
say. Regretting her alcohol consumption, she pulled her hand
away from Henri's and tried propping her elbows on the table,
her head cradled in her palms. She looked directly in his eyes.
"Go on."

"We are the same since we help support our beloved artists
and keep the community going. I do wish you would stay
longer." He reached for her hand, and she cautiously released
one of her chin supports to clasp his hand above their glasses.

He continued. "I realize I might not be arduous enough for
you, for I know I am not much of a man to give to a woman. But
there are things that are more important than just the mere act
of making love." He paused with a sigh before saying, "I would
give you my soul."

Deidre was at a loss for words. Here was the main man she
was sent to study. He was a key focus of the Bohemian move-

ment. She could not let this happen. She was to observe, but not interfere too greatly with her main subject, especially one so famous. Get close, but not too close was the Time Council's rule drilled into her. She was to observe without causing her subjects to change as a direct result from her interactions. Watch, observe, and notice.

She had been careful around Henri. All of her dalliances had been chosen with equal care. She had become part of the group to benefit from actual participation in the artistic revolution to be studied. But she couldn't continue on with her research and jump to her next assignment without gathering the potent energy through sex. It was the thing most found in abundance through time. Sex was always available. But she had to be careful whom it was with. Never someone too famous. She didn't want to totally change history. Never get too close to your subjects.

She was getting too close to Henri. She would have to pull away slowly. History could be affected. She couldn't live with herself if she let Henri Lautrec be dissuaded from his destiny. She had to let him down easily.

"My dear Henri." This time she looked down, and he knew. She could feel it as he began to loosen his hold of her hand. The joining was less intense. However, he did not let go.

"I am quite flattered." She looked up and held his gaze. He deserved the truth of her feelings, if not her mission. "I do consider you a very, dear and close friend. I do not need to share your bed to have the attraction to you as a person. I do consider you the greatest artist of your time."

She saw no real hope in his eyes, just an understanding. She would be biologically younger than he, if there wasn't the play of time between them. His early thirties age was ancient for this time. Her modest late twenties was just a drop in the pool of years humans achieved in her time. He couldn't know what would befall him in the next few years. She couldn't let him deviate.

He did flush a little from her comments. "I understand." He looked down for a moment and licked his lips. Then looked back into her eyes. "I don't know if that is true. I don't see myself as a great artist. I am quite happy to create my art, see the life behind closed doors, and spend it visiting with the people I hold dear in Montmartre."

He kissed both of her hands and held them as he held her gaze. "Do go to London and continue your love for art. I will miss your undeniable opinion on how painting is the true form to create color. But I leave you with the argument that lithographs can create designs of form that rival even sculpture." He laughed at this. "Even if our friend Gaston will never agree."

She rose now, steadying herself against the table because of the wine. He reached out quickly to take her arm. "I'm fine, Henri. I should be off now. It has been a long night." She knew it was time to get some sleep before her last day. She still had others to visit, others to observe before her departure.

Plus, this new development in her association with Henri Toulouse-Lautrec could endanger the time continuum. She couldn't let any involvement happen that would prevent his immediate future. Though she wished she could warn him of the disease which, within the span of a few years, would kill him.

It was for the best to move on. She could feel her impact on the people in her area of study was starting to evolve past the point of observation, and more into becoming one of them.

She was startled as she was revived from her thoughts. Henri had guided her toward the doorway, the volume of the conversations dropping behind them as they passed through the door. "Do you think you can make it up the stairway to your apartment?" he whispered, guiding her to the back stairs.

She nodded. She would not allow the world to spin. The Bohemian influence was starting to rub off on her. She had lost count of how much wine she'd had. "I'm fine, dear Henri. I can make it up. It isn't the first time that I've found my way from the café. I do thank you so much for your conversation tonight. I find your 'little parties' are enjoyable events."

"They are always better when you are at them, Deidre, my darling. Now, up the stairs and to your door." The stairway was near the back of the café. He got her to the second floor and accompanied her to the door of her apartment. "Best to make sure you get to safety with no mishaps."

"You are the gentleman, Henri." She looked for the key in her small, velvet purse attached to her wrist. Catching the tassel it was attached to, she placed it into the keyhole. Turning slowly, the click announced her entrance to safety, for herself and Henri's future. She kissed him on the cheek and grasped his hand again. "Thank you, good friend. I'll be here for at least a few more days."

There was a spark in Henri's eyes. "Perhaps the one painting I've been planning. It is time."

She nodded. She'd promised to pose for him. But how to without creating too much of a ripple in the future? Leaving now would make a good safe exit. But she would love to see his brushwork or maybe a sketch. "Perhaps in the next few days. I'll be in the café most of the time, or up here packing."

"If you can stay away from the painter and the sculptor." He tipped his hat her way as she gave him a big slap on the arm. At this, Henri Lautrec turned, leaving her as he eased himself back down the hallway with his cane. Funny, she hadn't noticed he leaned so much on it. It was so much a part of him that it wasn't noticeable except for the extra tap now and then.

She stepped into her apartment and proceeded to ready herself for her next journey. It was needed more than she expected.

Three

Cobblestones were quite treacherous when running in heels. Deidre had to take the chance if she was to have enough time to see Gaston before the scheduled time-jump. She had to finish what had started last night. The final rendezvous would give her the needed energy for the jump, and the final piece to her research report on the artists of Montmartre. She had to have the sculptor use her for his masterpiece. It was her last chance to see the way things were sculpted before the digital revolution and three-dimensional scanning.

She knocked on the door of the small studio. It was not much, just a small room next to a brothel and café, and it had a small open-air garden in the back that Gaston used for most of his subjects to pose. He said it was all about the light. He enjoyed having the light directly on his subjects' faces and bodies so he could more fully discern their contours.

She had come in her favorite red silk dress highlighted with black trim. Her hat had black lace and a dyed ostrich plume. Her black gloves were matched to her black corset. It was her color of choice most of the time when she could buy it. She couldn't take much with her each time-jump. She always managed a shopping trip after jumping to a new location.

She straightened her corset and set her hat back as the door swung open. Gaston was sprinkled with bits of plaster and dust. White powder was all over his trousers. His shirt hung open to expose a well-formed chest. She couldn't help but lower her eyes once to take in his midriff. She hoped he hadn't started drinking yet. He was gentler before the wine began to flow.

"Gaston, I've come for my appointment." She clasped her purse between her hands, giving him a demure look. She knew the people on the street could watch the houses to blackmail the patrons that might enter the studios. Luckily, she had no connections to exploit. But she had to look like she was following the pretext of hiding her actions.

Good research was done by fitting in with the assumed culture of the period. After almost three months of study, she was feeling like she knew how a Victorian woman felt. Even in the absence of the twenty-second-century technology and amenities, she could grow to like it here. But in the end, she knew that's why the time limits were set. One could fall in love with the past. It would be dangerous to allow her actions to make many changes. Staying behind longer than assigned was too much of a risk.

"Come in, my flower, I have been expecting you." Gaston's sweeping gesture commanded her to step forward. She nodded acceptance and strode through the doorway. Gaston quickly closed the door and took her in his arms. He had a strong kiss that bordered on much too wet for her tastes. But his hands were his specialty.

She stayed locked in his embrace for a few moments. When they drew apart, she looked into his blue eyes. One thing about artists: they all liked to wear their hair long. She undid the tie and let his blond hair fall around his shoulders. His neckline and chest were accented by his open shirt.

She stroked the center of his chest and grabbed his waist. "Where do you want me to pose, mon cher?"

He kissed her again, but rejected her initial urgings to continue. "Come, I must finish the statue first. I must refine the angles of your hips, legs, and waist. And I want you in this light. However, when the sun goes down…" He kissed her again, and then led her to a cushioned bench in the garden. Honeysuckle intertwined on a trellis behind. She lowered herself to the cushioned bench. The cushion's royal blue velvet brought out the red of her dress and lips as she got into position.

"Would you like me to pose with my clothes on or not? I need direction." She pouted after her last sentence. Unable to resist, Gaston came toward her. "I will need them off. But I can help." He stooped to help remove her shoes first, then pulled her up and with agile fingers undid her dress. She stepped out of the dress and waited for Gaston to remove her corset. The release that allowed her to breathe was almost better than an orgasm. But Gaston was more interested in tracing her curves under each breast, down her flat stomach to her waist. She let her corset drop to the floor.

"Your curves will bring my nymph to life."

With a laugh, Deidre removed each stocking, to the avid eyes of Gaston. Blue eyes burst with longing as she tossed each stocking to him. She slowly wiggled out of her pantaloons, at last free of the nineteenth-century confines to her body.

"How should I lie down?" she asked as she began to lower herself back down on her perch.

Gaston stood transfixed. Then, he bent forward and cupped the back of her head, slowly lowering her down on her back. He took her one hand and placed it behind her head, then pulled her hip forward, tilting her body toward him, her knees bent, one slightly more than the other. Her breasts pressed together as he retrieved a pillow to place under her head. Her free arm draped down in front of her as she looked toward him. He backed up to his stool and statue block.

"How should my face be?"

"Natural. Always natural."

He began working the stone. One nice thing about this time period was the ability to be the human form that was studied. It presented the best opportunity to study the artist's technique. She had to sit for hours at a time watching him. She wasn't sure how much she was absorbing from his work, but she knew it would definitely be a benefit to the Time Institution's archives. Her implant recorded every move he made, even when she didn't understand the artist's techniques.

The scent of honeysuckle seemed to rest atop the smells of plaster dust and wood, creating an intoxicating blend of scents. She knew her job was to hold still, but posing for sculptors was the hardest. They took the longest to get the needed angle or form to copy. But Gaston worked fast. His hands were in good condition for it.

On occasion, her mind would wander, as would her visual focus, and he would remind her to look at him. After a while, she started to ease her position. "Gaston, parts of me are falling asleep. Really, I'll need a break soon." She transformed her mouth into the perfect pout that often charmed the men when she needed to get their attention. The sun was going down. She had until midnight tonight to get her bracelet charged. She was running out of time, and she wanted one last night in the Bohemian scene to say her final good-byes.

"Just a bit more, chèrie. I need to work the area around your stomach, and then I'll be done. I am finished with your face for now. You may move it, but not the rest of your body."

It was a cue for her to rebel. She started by moving her nose slightly. Then closed one eye, then the other. Gaston gave her a quick look. "Mon Dieu." And then returned to his work. She continued this act of rebellion by sticking out her tongue. Then, smiled.

"I can't do anything with you after an hour. You always have trouble staying still." He walked over and captured her mouth with another kiss. He pulled the edges of her lips slowly into his mouth. This was new. She returned the action to find the match of pressure created a new sensation. Interesting. She wrapped her arms around him as he moved on top of her.

"I've been wanting to do this since you walked in the door, ma chèrie."

"Why did you wait?" She sounded sincere. Yet, she couldn't hide the note of bedevilment.

"The light, ma chèrie, the light was just right. We had to use the moment for art."

"Now is the moment for love," she whispered.

He answered with another kiss as she lay back on the cushioned bench. Gaston started to use those talented hands to caress the upper part of her body, beginning with her neck, then moving his hands over her breasts. She felt her nipples perk into peaks at his electric touch. He traced down her abdomen to caress around her hips and held her in an embrace. They leaned together for another kiss, holding and feeling their bodies mold into each other.

He loosened his grip and she arched her back, letting her hair fall to the floor. "Your curves and lines are the perfection of a woman, my love."

She sat up with a smile. "I want to see your lines now."

He stood up and let his trousers drop to the floor. He was Atlas at full mast. She stood up to trace his chest, nuzzle his nipples, and run her hands up his back. He picked her up and carried her to the straw mattress he used for sleeping. Lowering her to the pallet he came down upon her, never breaking eye contact.

"Now, Gaston. I can't wait for you any longer."

He eased inside her. Back and forth, he thrust into her, building a rhythm. She felt the rise of excitement and wanted to hold Gaston in the right place. She wrapped her legs around him, feeling him move over the spot that gave her the most pleasure. Each movement was leading to an explosive power that could only be released one way. It burst with waves of rapture rolling through her very being. He joined her after one final thrust. They climaxed together.

She felt the vibration behind her left ear letting her know the time energy crystal had been filled.

Gaston cradled her in his arms. She played with his hair until he was ready to release her. She enjoyed the moment as long as she could. Time-jumps always made her feel queasy, and it was so hard to make the initial connections. She savored the intimate touch of Gaston tracing the shape of her breast. She would miss him. It was the hardest part of her job, making new connections after each time-jump. She always savored the final moments before her good-byes. It would be a while before she would be able to connect this way again.

They must have nodded off. When she opened her eyes, the sunlight through the windows was almost gone. She had just this evening to say her good-byes. It would be her last observation. She wanted it to be at the Moulin de la Galette. Most of the Bohemian artists she had met and observed would be there. At least, she was hoping for that tonight. She wanted to be present for the best artistic gathering on her last night in Paris.

She moved her body, startling Gaston awake. She looked down and stroked his arm as he regained consciousness. He buried his face in her breasts, grabbing her middle. "This is the best pillow I've ever woken upon." He looked up at her mischievously. "Should we try some more posing, or do you have other things in mind?"

She wrapped her arms around his neck. "I am actually hungry, Gaston. You've worked up my appetite. Since this is my last night, why don't we go see who is at the Moulin de la Galette? I am craving a *ginguet* to salute my last night in Paris."

Grabbing her, and rolling beneath her, he asked, "Are you sure? It's your turn to be on top."

"I'm sure," she said as she braced up against him. "I know how big your appetite can be, but this time, mine is for food."

He kissed her, helping her up, and led her to where her clothes had been discarded. "I'll grab something to make myself presentable to the public." He picked up her dress and held it up to her. "This color makes you look like such a fine woman. You are almost too refined for a ravishing red dress like this."

She grabbed the dress from him. "I want to make a splash on my last night. I want to be noticeable, make an exit worthy of the stage. It's my way to let everyone know that I'm leaving, and a little insight to how you all have affected me." She smiled before continuing. "I don't think I would have worn a red such as this before I met you or any of the other Bohemians that have influenced me."

"We love to corrupt the young. I am glad you have joined our cause." He sealed her membership with a kiss. Then, he swatted her on the ass. "Come now, we have an evening of memories to make. We must do that clothed, for society's sake."

"Of course. Someday, society may think otherwise." She smiled with the knowledge that it was partly true. She still wore clothes in her time, but the sharing of one's body had no limits. She felt in some ways, things had come a long way.

Gaston didn't take long to present himself in a handsome black coat, dress shirt, and brown trousers that weren't covered in sculpting residue. His hair was tied back with a black cord, and he wore a gentleman's top hat. He had shined himself up.

She looked him up and down. "I appreciate the clean up, Gaston."

"Anything for my dear Deidre. We will transform this town in an evening. We are unstoppable." He offered her his arm. She took it, wrapping her hand around his to join at her waist. This would be the best night of her research so far, for it would be her last in Montmartre.

Four

She glided on Gaston's arm through the streets of Montmartre to the Moulin de la Galette. She was drinking in the sights of the quarter, the laughter from the cafés, the prostitutes in the alleys, and most of all, the man on her arm she would miss. Their eyes met as they came to the garden entry. After a quick kiss, Gaston turned to the maître d' to get a table.

They were taken to a part of the garden patio where she saw many faces she recognized. A writer named Bertram gave her a nod, but seemed a bit distant. It might have been the fact she was on Gaston's arm that made him wary. The territorial behavior of men often baffled her.Bertram edged forward as they sat down at their table. He nodded to both. "Gaston! Deidre! It is good to see you again. I have heard the news. We are losing our flower of Montmartre. What garden are you planning to grow in next?"

"London," she answered. "With all the rain, I'm hoping to blossom."

"Oh, I know our flower will never wilt, in spite of the lack of English sun. Why leave here, the glory that is the radiance of the new age? But you'd best be watchful how many bees might be pollinating." Bertram's teasing was a bit harsh. She realized it might have been the fact he had lost out in the battle for her attention. She didn't need to study a writer for this assignment, and hadn't pursued his advances for her interest. Bitterness did not make his boyish features attractive.

"Come now, Bertram. Our Deidre would never fail to find a way to bloom. We must give her a party before she leaves."

"I'm sure you've had no problem making sure she was plowed and seeded, Gaston."

Gaston stood up. Some of the other patrons stopped at the raising of voices. Carefully, the surrounding crowd moved back to give room for the show certain to follow.

Deidre stood raising a hand for both to stop their posturing. "Please, Bertram. Join us. Things can often be solved by a glass of wine. Let us have peace restored. I would insist, since this is my last night."

Gaston tugged at his coat and adjusted his sleeves. "Deidre, you restore my faith in women. You are too gracious a woman to be allowing an ingrate writer to shatter the peace of your last evening."

"I am hoping that he is a good sport and enjoys the free wine." Deidre smiled, flashing a dimple, as she gestured to another seat at their table.

Bertram grabbed the sides of his coat and answered, "Free wine would let anyone forget their differences." He sat down with them as the waiter brought over a bottle.

"In fact," continued Deidre, "I think more things could be solved by simply discussing them over wine."

"Wars could be averted with full barrels as well," Gaston joined into the discussion helping to change the subject.

Bertram laughed, "Yes, Gaston. If all the soldiers sat at a table and each had a glass, they would soon forget what they were fighting over."

Gaston poured a glass for each of them. "To Deidre's last night, may London's fog not dim the brightness of the lights of Paris."

The clink of glasses was followed by Deidre's answer, "And let the light of Paris guide me through my times in London." As they drank, she noticed Henri in the corner sketching away. He kept looking at their table. The cloud of smoke wafting from the cigars and pipes created a haze in the garden. He nodded her way, and she raised her glass to him. She tried to gesture for him to join. He shook his head no, motioning to his sketchpad.

As the night wore on, he continued with the occasional look in her direction. He seemed in thrall of trying to capture the moment of a French Galette. He was famous for these sketches. She felt it a shame that he would not enjoy the full reign of his popularity. So few artists were ever appreciated while they were alive.

She raised her glass to him again and smiled back. In the end, it looked like Henri had gotten a chance to sketch her after all. However, he was too far away for her to see all of his work. She knew if she left the scene, she'd ruin the moment for him. So, she returned to the conversation, fulfilled that her research was a success. But really, it was worth the effort to see Henri smile.

—⚬—

Deidre felt as though the world had dimmed as she made her way down the stairway, through the closed café, holding her small bag. She didn't need much. Most of the things she needed she would buy in the new time period. But she was going to miss her scarlet dress. The clothing was the most important thing that helped her fit into each time period. She would have to find new clothes in London or at least some passable basics on the way after she jumped.

She moved to the bar and left her room key in the mail drop for Monsieur Fortecourt. He shouldn't have trouble finding another person to rent the room. People were always moving in and out of Montmartre.

The early morning met Deidre with an overcast sky and damp streets. She made her way to the stable where her carriage was stored. She had to wake the stableman, and gave him more than just the storage fee to keep quiet about her departure. She wanted her exit from Paris to be discreet as possible.

She was directed to the stable that held her time vehicle. The time vehicle was in the form of a carriage, the best way to disguise it. It had to be something that no one would suspect in this time. Holograms and matter projections made it possible. She didn't know the exact mechanics on how it worked. She was only trained on how to work the controls plus simple repairs in the event she got stuck. She wasn't an engineer. If something completely malfunctioned, she'd be out of luck or have to be directed to a left behind time machine for emergencies. They could be sent back and left for stranded timeanauts.

The main bits were built to last through one large jump back and then small jumps forward powered by her bracelet. It made it easier to move through time if she did it in small jumps. The initial jump was made back in time. It was a large burst of power by the Time Council.

After that initial push back in time, a timeanaut could only move forward, toward their original time period, as mandated by the Council. She had so wanted to go back to save James. But she knew the power needed was beyond her capability and it was against Council law. He was lost. Forever.

She reached for the door. The stableman helped to open it so she could get footing to climb within. As she stepped up, black cushioned seats were the only thing visible to the stableman. She could see the whole console to operate the time mechanisms. Her implant allowed her to. When she closed the door behind her, she waited for the liveryman to leave before she pushed the button to activate the vehicle.

Taking the bracelet from her arm, Deidre unlocked the jewel from its center. It clicked and fell into her palm. She pushed it into the slot near the top of the console. Everything lit up at once as she looked over the touchpad controls. She slid and touched the controls with expert practice. A driver was projected onto the seat, with a black horse tacked up and attached into the harness.

Time-jumps had to be done separately from the actual travel to a destination. To get to a place in a different time, she had to go to that time first. Once there, her journey would continue along the physical plane. Time travel worked in moving to a new time, not a new space.

She set the vehicle into its initial start up, punching in the coordinates that would take her out of the city on a country road to her jump location outside Calais. It was safer to travel to her jump location unnoticed, and the country roadways were the best for not colliding with other vehicles. She knew she had to get out of the city for her jump. She didn't want to jump into the space of some other person or thing when she arrived at her new destination. Jumping was safer away from other people and places.

She punched in a year and date. May 1, 1914. Once she jumped, she knew she couldn't go back. She pushed the engage icon and heard the driver hologram whistle to the projected horse. At the whistle, the stableman opened the doors, and Deidre's carriage rolled out of the stable toward the future.

She flipped back the small curtains that lined the window. The streets were mostly deserted. She would have a while to enjoy the last sights of Paris. Sacred-Coeur rose in the distance as she rounded a bend. She was going to miss the white church that towered over the area, even though it didn't hold much sway over Montmartre.

The bumps and movements of the carriage would keep sleep at bay, even after her long night with Gaston. She hadn't had the heart to do much more than kiss him good-bye. She was going to miss him far more than she had imagined.

The wine had gotten to her head, and she had told him so. It was enough that she had filled the charge band and could finally leave for her next destination. She understood why Philippe had acted as he did. She would have to add it to her report. Each new jump was taking a toll on her heart and soul. She couldn't allow that. Timeanauts had to stay neutral. Connections were forbidden. It was just too dangerous.

She could remember the briefing before her first mission. She was told to get in the middle of an artistic movement. The best observation was done when involved in the movement, but not directly involved. Observation from within was key, but it was difficult to find the balance. She was expected to get close, but not too close.

But her heart had gotten too attached to James. She knew how dangerous being a timeanaut could be. They tried to keep a separation between them, to be somewhat professional. But timeanauts often had to use each other to charge their bracelets.

She sighed. Her head felt too muddled with thoughts. She had tried to not fall for James. But knew now she'd lost the battle. She must have loved him. She could feel that now that he was gone.

She leaned against the side wall, letting herself be relaxed by the movement of the carriage. The crack of the driver's whip and whistles gave realism to the time vehicle. Inside, she watched the digital map track her distance down the road toward the jump. She had over forty miles—and a few more hours—until it was time. Her last few days had worn her out, and she was mentally and physically weary. She hoped her mind would rest and she would find sleep, but it wasn't to be.

Her heart ached to be with Gaston again. A tear escaped from her closed eyes and slid down her cheek. She had let him get too close to her too. It couldn't happen again. It was for their safety as well as her own. Never get too close. Never get too involved. The past must be observed, but never directly changed. A shadow of her past drifted across her mind. Like what had happened with James. She could never get that close again.

She pushed her mind to other things. Her thoughts drifted, matching the bouncing of the carriage. Her research was rewarding, to finally meet and interact with some of history's famous artists. But saying good-bye was the hardest part. Sometimes, she would be amused that she was becoming part of their great legend, if a small one. But it was the best way to find out the truth of their artistry. Love had no place in her research. Sometimes when she left, she felt the chill of loneliness blanket her soul.

She understood why her occupation wasn't allowed more than five years of travel time. She'd logged in almost two years now, and knew she was in the middle of her career. Could she endure the separation from her own time for another three years? Fifteen-year jumps made it possible. With one burst of energy to the past, she was at the whim of producing her own energy to return home to her time. The only way was forward in smaller jumps, fifteen years at a time. It was the allowance determined by the Time Council, and most timeanaut training involved isolation periods to get used to the simpler life of the past.

Whole training classes were dedicated to life skills lost in the future, like cooking, cleaning, mending, and daily chores. She had been schooled in a lot of the lost skills. But nothing prepared you for the real thing. It was the experience of being with the people that really made it the most difficult. You could fall in love with them.

Her mind started to drift back to Gaston again. She imagined tracing her finger down his chest again. Then stroking to feel the definition of each pectoral, finally sliding down around his waist. He would not have been able to take more, and would be kissing her right now. She closed her eyes slowly, imagining his lips on hers.

God, she hated this. Hated having to leave them all. Another jump. More she had to leave behind. James's face swam in her memory followed by Gaston's. She shook her head. She had to concentrate on her next mission. If she checked her carriage archive, she could brush up on the next assignment before making the jump.

She tapped the console screen. Her next mission subject came up on the screen. A picture of a simple-looking man with a slim, long face and round eyes appeared, his name and occupation printed below: Henri Gaudier, Vorticist sculptor, involved in the early days of Vorticism. Died in 1915 in the trenches of World War I. More instructions appeared under his picture.

Her new mission was to somehow become part of the group of artists known as the Vorticists, through parties and such, and then find her way to him to study his technique and style. She was to make contact at a restaurant called the Restaurant de la Tour Eiffel where the artists were known to gather. Her undercover name was to be Deidre Thompson, an American heiress on a European tour. The rest of how she was to accomplish her mission was up to her.

She looked at his photograph again. He had a very long nose, proud angular cheekbones, and thin small lips. Not another sculptor. She scrolled through more of the file. There was the main published newsletter by the group. It was called *Blast* magazine, the centerpiece for the movement. A picture of the first published issue with a bright pink cover appeared. It said it contained the manifesto of the group. Dated June 20, 1914, it was the first clue on who to associate with.

She looked at all of the names and cross-referenced. Only two were women, Helen Saunders and Jessica Dismorr. Jessica resided in Hampstead. Deidre wondered what circles she would need to introduce herself into to get an invitation to a party with the major players of the movement.

She browsed through more material, quickly starting to lose concentration as her weariness caught up with her. She hadn't been up this early in ages. Bohemians didn't rise with the sun. She could just take a break for a moment. She rubbed her eyes and curled up on the bench. The movement of the carriage was so lulling.

There was a three-beep alarm. Three minutes until the time-jump. How had she fallen asleep? She sat up and stretched, flexing her legs, her knees stiff from being curled up for so long. She looked out the window to see a fog creeping over the French countryside. She must be nearing the coast.

The jostle of the carriage slowed as it neared the position of the jump. The land stretched with fields of wheat in all directions. France was living up to its reputation of being the breadbasket of Europe. The carriage slowed and stopped. There was another beep, and a countdown on the panel. She braced herself for the queasy feeling that always accompanied a time-jump. "Three, two, one."

Nausea and black out. Limitless falling and then nothing. She came to and felt a familiar stillness inside the carriage. A wind was blowing outside, hard and heavy as if a storm was approaching.

"Beginning carriage transformation to 1914 vehicle configuration." The humanistic computer voice echoed within the confines of her compartment. "New transformation will begin in five, four, three, two, one." There was a slight vibration in the walls. "Vehicle exterior design complete. Waiting for timeanaut instruction to continue."

On the monitor was the design for her 1914 vehicle, a 1914 Napier T78 coupe in a deep racing-green color, cream highlights, and green leather interior. Her driver was now in the chauffeur seat up front, while she reclined in the enclosed rear cabin. Windows began to fog due to the outside temperature change. "Initiating transportation to London, One Percy Street."

She answered the time vehicle's computer. "Go." Her voice was absorbed by the rich leather interior. The car started down the gravel road. The car wound down the road to Port de Calais where a steamer ferry was docked. A line of other opulent cars formed on the pier. As she observed the people in the area, she felt out of place with her current dress. She hit the panel and outside cameras zoomed in on a sign posting the ferry departure times. It said three in the afternoon marked out in chalk. The ship was going to wait until the change in tide to depart.

The arms on the clock next to the timetable read eight o'clock. Seven hours should give her enough time to find some kind of dress. She didn't want to be too out of fashion. She wouldn't fit in. She let the time vehicle drive to the dock as she pressed into the matter transformer to duplicate money for 1914. She could create gold as well if money wasn't used, but currency was always so much easier.

When she arrived at the dock, she was at the end of a long line of cars. She stepped out onto a wooden walkway. Closing the door, she instructed, "Go forward" to her driver. Cranes were loading other vehicles onto the ship. The car moved forward to the line of cars loading on the dock. She asked a nearby dock-hand where to go to book passage. "That way, madam, it's the path to the office." She followed the dock to the ticket office and bought a first-class passenger ticket and freight fees for her car.

She hurried into the cobblestone streets, avoiding bicycles and more carriages. Dodging quickly, she moved to the safety of the paved sidewalk. She followed the flow of people along the cobblestone streets. It was good to see less mud and more civilized progress. She went as fast as she dared in her shoes. With a low heel, progress was treacherous if she moved too quickly.

She progressed through a main avenue, looking for the signs of a dressmaker. The women she passed in the street sported long pencil skirts with a wide variety of blouses and jackets. If she couldn't find a fully equipped dressmaker, a blouse or tailor might be the next best thing.

She walked into a blouse-maker's shop. There was a skirt and blouse she could exchange for her older dress. The modern styles still included long skirts and differing tops. Wearing her new blouse, she kept the jacket. The skirt she had would work until she could shop at a department store in London. She had heard so much about this time, with the retail and manufacturing still in its infancy. Some of her purchases she had to scan for the archive.

She noticed hats were still in fashion. She went into a hat shop and bought one to give herself more character, and to fit in. Its elegant, wide felt brim fitted with feathers and ribbon made her feel ready for the days ahead. She admired herself in the mirror while the shopkeeper looked on. Nodding, she paid for her purchases. Her older shoes would have to do. She had a boat to catch.

Deidre walked out onto the street feeling like a new woman. A change of clothes always changed one's mood. She made good time in getting back to the ferry. As she walked onto the first-class deck, looking at the view, she felt as if she were being followed. She turned to notice the same, strange man from the café in Montmartre, staring at her from across the deck. He was smoking a cigarette, dressed for this time, with a bowler hat and black suit. His eagle-eye glance matched hers. How could the same man from fifteen years ago be following her?

She dodged the approaching man by heading into the ship's café where she ordered a light lunch. Her stomach needed some attention after the day's events. She made sure she kept an eye on the man, his cloud of smoke trailing behind as he continued his promenade.

She must have imagined it. She hadn't eaten at all in the morning, and decided her hunger, on top of the long journey, was playing tricks with her eyes. But he did have the same dashing look as before. His eyes. They bored into her like they did in the café in Paris.

She stayed mostly in the café, sipping an Italian soda, during the crossing. The movement of the rocking boat made her not want any wine. The soda steadied her stomach. Sea travel never agreed with her. It was so different from the modes of travel in the future. Being on the surface of water or land to travel was just not done in her time.

If she left the confines of the café, she made a point to stay with groups of people. She didn't see the strange man again until she was heading to the restroom. She almost bumped into him going down the stairway.

"Pardon me," his voice held an unusual accent she couldn't place.

"Yes, *monsieur*." That was it. She retreated to the powder room and looked into the mirror. Her heart beat fast. She didn't like being noticed unless it was in her plan. He did look like the same man in the café in Paris. The same blue eyes had stared back at her. She shook her head. No, maybe it was just her imagination. He might be a relative of the other man's, after all, just on business to London. But she could have sworn it was the same man.

The Dover Harbor looked like a sanctuary to her as they entered through the barrier walls. The roughness of the seas subsided. She would be happy to finally be off the boat. She decided that a short stay in a small hotel would be restorative before she made her way to London. Maybe she could get a good night's sleep before the real work began.

She didn't notice him follow her from the docks.

Five

Deidre made it through the customs line exiting the ferry in time to see her Napier lifted by crane to the docks. Somehow, just looking at her time vehicle made her feel reassured. Adjusting to each new period took a while. The time vehicle was the only constant. No matter how much virtual studying she did, it wasn't the same as traveling to a new place and time. Nothing prepared you fully.

She boarded the Napier, quickly hiding in the passenger cabin, feeling locked and safe once inside. "Head into town to a hotel."

The computer voice asked, "Specify type of hotel, please."

"Comfortable, one bed in room. Toilets down the hall okay." She paused to consider. "A specialty of chips and mushy peas in the restaurant. I want to try those."

The holographic driver brought the engine to life and rolled down the street. She decided to put the strange man in the back of her thoughts and get on with the rest of her mission. After all, it was impossible she was being followed through time. Or was it?

The streets were wet from a fresh rain. The Napier splashed through puddles, but wasn't able to dodge the few potholes scattered throughout the muddy road. She arrived at a comfortable-looking inn with a restaurant next door. The Napier stopped in front of the restaurant and she stepped out, then told the driver, "Go," and it pulled through the carriage entrance to park in the back stable area. Her vehicle had basic driver interaction if necessary, and should be able to arrange itself as if the chauffeur were really driving and storing the vehicle.

As Deidre walked into the restaurant, she realized how cold it had been outside. Her hands were quite cold and she wished she'd bought a muff or gloves. This new assignment might be much chillier than she'd planned for. Folding her hands within her sleeves to keep warm, she sat quietly at a table waiting for service. As she waited, she noticed the horse medal decorations, wooden tables, chairs, and large wooden bar. The ale choices and specials were written in chalk on a board near the bar. Not too many of the tables seemed occupied. She hoped that only reflected the time of day, not the quality of the food.

A man came through a narrow opening from the back, smiling as he cleaned a cup. "Welcome, miss. What may I get ya?"

She looked over the specials board and answered, "Fish and chips with mushy peas. I would love some of that."

The man looked puzzled as he nodded. "Where are you from?" he asked as he finished the glass. "Unusual to see such a pretty thing as you traveling alone."

"I've just arrived from Paris. I'm heading to London to visit my relatives. Though I have to say, it's my first time in England.

I am looking forward to my first dish of English food." She gave him one of her smiles. They often disarmed men and got them to do what she wanted. She didn't want to seem the meek type, and definitely not a target for unsavory attention, unless she wanted it.

"I will be glad to represent Britain in the best that we have to share. Which isn't the food, I might add. I'll suggest a nice cup of tea. Makes British food taste one hundred times better."

"I'll have that to start, then." She gave him a wicked smile. "I do so need to adjust to the British way of doing things."

He gave her a wink, adding, "I'll hurry it up then. Don't want to keep a woman waiting."

While the man went to fix her tea, she observed more of her surroundings. The dim light coming from the windows allowed her to see a few lone travelers, mostly men, sitting at tables or at the bar. She expected to see the stranger looking at her from a corner. Deidre discerned the people walking by the window outside. They seemed to be having polite conversation, intent on their own business, without looking around. She was startled when the waiter returned.

"Here's the best tea we have. On the house, for such a lovely lady. We don't get many of you often enough. Your food will be right up." He went back through a door to the kitchen. She returned to watching the people on the street. A boy chasing another ran up against the window, tagged the other boy, and dashed off. Men walked by with bowler hats, umbrellas in hand. Women and men strolled by on their own hidden business, too busy to look at the lone woman watching things she'd only seen in pictures and holograms.

The streets were crowded with traffic. A bicycle sprinted between some wagons and a carriage, traveling down another road. In the distance, ships and steamers entered the harbor or prepared to leave. Moored boats had sailors scurrying about to ready or disembark. Seabirds circled the leavings from fishing boats.

Her trance was broken when the waiter clanked her plate onto the table. "The best cod in Britain. The best way to introduce yourself to fish and chips, miss." He tipped his flat cap to her.

Her translator must be giving her an American accent to help her fit in with her background story. She might need to reprogram it later into a British accent, and even match a region of London. But first things first, she was hungry. She bit into the fish and savored the fresh taste. The food in the past had tremendous flavor. The lack of toxins and additives always surprised her. She ate so quickly that a small burp escaped her. Looking about to see if anyone had noticed, she washed the food down with her tea and left a shilling on the table.

"'Night, miss." She nodded to the helpful waiter and ran into another man coming through the door. As she looked up, she looked into his eyes. The ones that had bored into her were deep blue with flecks of green. His black hair was swept back under his bowler, and he quickly bowed to her. It was him. The man that had been following her. "I'm sorry," she whispered.

He tipped his hat to her. "A thousand pardons. I seem to keep running into you." His smile sent shivers down her back. He was very attractive. She hadn't seen him up close long enough until now. It shocked her that she felt breathless.

"It's fine, sir. It happens when one travels abroad."

"Of course." He bowed to her, and she used the gesture as a moment to make her escape. He was unnerving her in a way she hadn't expected. And he had been following her. She was sure of it. But doubt crept in. Was it really the same man?

She left the restaurant and followed the path to the inn's main entrance. She stepped through the door and heard a bell. A woman looked up from behind the check-in desk. "Welcome, miss. What can I do for you today?"

"A room for one please."

She checked in and went up to her room. She was exhausted. The day had been doubly long and full of surprises. The mysterious man was starting to be a little too noticeable. Whenever she traveled, she only wanted to be noticed when it was needed. Who was he? Did he really follow her from 1899 or was it just a coincidence? The idea kept buzzing through her head as she lay wide awake.

It could all be a mistake. But somewhere inside her, she wished he would talk to her. She kept thinking of his eyes on her. She wasn't sure why the loneliness stirred in her. It could have been the new jump, new assignment, new everything. The toll of the jumps must have been wearing on her. Losing James had been the start. Since she'd been without him, she had lost herself in the missions. Trying to enjoy the research was a distraction from what hurt inside. She was alone without him.

As she finally crawled into bed, her thoughts drifted to the mysterious man. Would he appear again? Was he really following her? She wasn't sure if she was going to find the answers. All she could do was continue with her mission and see what happened. All roads lead to Rome, or London in this case. She figured that the old adage applied a little. Going to London was her way to find answers. If he were really following her, she would maybe see him again.

She'd have to keep her eyes open for him. The thought of seeing him again brought a flush to her face and between her legs. She missed having someone to be with. Her sculptor, the painter. James. She hated starting over. That was one of the more difficult aspects of her job. She was alone again.

She wasn't sure if she wanted to go it alone the rest of the way, but she didn't seem to have a choice. The mission had to be completed. She had to jump forward to the Time Council's choice of subjects until she made it all the way back. She thought of the mysterious man one more time. What would it be like to be close to him? Her thoughts filled with the idea of a kiss from him. She sighed.

Her mind drifted to the last time she held James. His shouts for her to run, after he'd been stabbed by the highwayman, echoed in her mind. Her diving into the time vehicle, shouting the commands to jump forward as the other robbers tried to break in. She remembered looking through the back of the carriage. Seeing the scene of James collapsed in the dirt, a robber pulling the knife from his body wiping it on his clothes.

She cleared her mind. James couldn't be brought back. He'd given her the chance to get away and save herself. He was her partner. They had loved each other against all odds, maybe even against the Time Counsel's mandates. But he was gone now. She had to finish the mission. If for anyone, it should be for him. It was the least she could do for his sacrifice. Maybe she had to stop falling for men too. She promised herself. This was it. No more feelings. No more love.

She settled deeper into the pillow, smoothing the quilt that covered her. But her mind kept drifting to the beautiful eyes she had seen in the restaurant earlier.

London. The bustle of the town was intoxicating. Deidre looked through the window at wagons, carriages, and people doing a graceful dance of interplay with each other. Shouts rang among whips cracking. The clop of hooves amidst the din added to the overwhelming bustle. Bicycles wheeled through intersections as wagons proceeded down streets on the opposite side of the traffic from Paris. It was the chaos of the beginning of the industrial age, and she was bearing witness.

Victorian buildings ran up against each other. The design of rose and cream brick-striped patterns dominated corners of newer buildings. Streets joined in roundabouts. Often in the middle would be a statue. In the center, large circular sidewalks were crowded with pedestrians looking for safe ways to cross. Gas lamps lined the streets, giving the civility that would be needed for a city at night. Horse-drawn, double-decker wagons stopped at corners to let people exit to their destination.

Looking out the window, restaurants and hotels started to be more prevalent, along with rooms for rent. Painted on the sides of buildings were advertisements. "Mieux Three Guinea Stout," read one. Another read, "The Horseshoe Hotel. Restaurant. Grill Room. Large Rooms." As she neared Tottenham Court Road, she tried to read some of the signs to get an idea of where to stay for the night. It was becoming apparent that it might be difficult to keep her time vehicle in Central London. She may have to store it or stay further out in an outlying town. The city was just too crowded.

She had been studying up on the Vorticists during the ride to London, and decided to find lodgings outside of the bustle of London for the time being. If she found a place near Hampstead, it might make it easier to find a connection since some of the members lived near there.

She began searching through the database. A cross reference showed that Hampstead was a possible destination to store the car, gain temporary or permanent lodging, and set up possible connections. Several Vorticists had connections with the town. That would be a good place to start.

She entered Hampstead as her new destination. Three different hotels came up on her search. She selected a hotel in her database listed as connected to many writers and artists in the area. It was called the Castle Hotel. At least staying at the venue would give her a good central area to begin. Plus, a comfortable hotel would allow her to rest after her extensive travels.

The Napier headed down the streets of London toward Hampstead. She passed through parts of Camden Town, with hotels and rooms for rent. She noted the different locations of rooms available on her digital mapping system. She might need to check back just in case the hotel wasn't a long-term solution.

Traveling down Heath Street, she noticed the wider street with a middle section of trees shading the lane. Houses stood proudly together, braving the new century ahead. Corner buildings had the rounded ends that were so loved during the Victorian building phase. She was amazed to see them, new and spectacular instead of degraded and in ruin from her time.

As Deidre's vehicle pulled up in front of the two-story Castle Hotel, she watched the people in front of the Jack Straw's Castle, the pub next door, talking and enjoying a pint. She got out, looked for the hotel entrance, and went in. She noticed the appreciative looks from men as she walked through the entrance into the lobby. She was greeted by a friendly woman in her forties. "May I check you in?" She seemed quite hopeful in her tone.

"Oh yes. It has been a long journey. I really need a place to put my feet up." The irony of how long it had been made Deidre smile. "I could use a nice room for several days and storage for my automobile."

"Really. You have one of those new contraptions? I would love to see it."

"I'd be happy to show you, especially after I've had a moment to change and ready for dinner. It's quite a nice gift," here she thought quickly. "From my father. He has sent me abroad."

"Oh, you must be American then. Come to see Europe I imagine. Have you come alone?"

She frowned at this. It was amazing how time periods limited women's mobility. It was hard to get used to. "My father says it builds character to travel abroad and make do for one's self. I have found that I meet more people that way."

The woman nodded and started making notes in her registration book. "Welcome then, miss. What may I call you, then?"

"Deidre Thompson."

"Welcome, Miss Thompson. I'm sure you will enjoy your stay in Hampstead Town."

Deidre nodded. She knew she would. The records showed she already had.

Six

Deidre's opportunity to make contact with the Vorticists presented itself two weeks into her stay, when she was seated for afternoon tea. A woman sitting alone at a hotel always attracts attention. In her case, it was a well-to-do Brit by the name of John Spencer. After making eye contact with her, he had approached her table and introduced himself, explaining he'd come to town to meet a friend who'd since been delayed. Deidre glanced around and determined he was alone. "So, when do you expect him?" she asked.

Spencer gave a sly smile and said, "Dare I say, it's the same old story. He and one of his associates are in need of some creative space. May I join you for some tea?"

After giving him an appraising look, she motioned for him to join her and flashed a demure smile his way. "Creative space? Is your friend a writer?"

"Of the worst kind." He glanced around, then lowered his voice to a conspiratorial whisper. "He's a poet."

"Really," she replied. "Would I know his name?"

"He's been to America, and has some minor publications. His name is Ezra Pound."

Deidre nodded in recognition of the name, but trying not to seem too eager to learn more about that, she said, "Well, enough about your friend. Tell me, what do you do for a living?" Always a safe topic to ask any man about in any time. She needed to choose her associations carefully to make the right connections.

"An old family business for the most part," he said. "We've branched out to buy a factory up north. Plus, a few investments overseas are paying off."

She took a sip of her tea. "Interesting. What type of factory?" She wanted to keep him talking and find some common ground to connect with. If she could get invited to a party with Ezra Pound and his friends, it would be a quick way into the Vorticists group.

"Mostly mills in Yorkshire. But I want Father to branch out."

Apparently in need of changing the subject, or maybe just trying to be gentlemanly, he said, "Tell me. Have you seen interesting things during your visit?"

"My visit? I guess my accent gave me away," she said.

He laughed and gave her a flirtatious wink.

"I have seen the most wonderful sorts of things," she said enthusiastically. "I'm sad to be nearing the end of my trip. I start back home soon." She sighed for emphasis. "I am so going to miss Europe. Paris was the most memorable of all." She smiled at that. She did truly miss Paris. It was a timeless city.

"What did you like the most?" He leaned forward to gain a better look at the cleavage revealed by her dress She did so love the inviting neck plunge the dress offered. With her hair up and hands gloved, the one arrow that pointed to the provocative spot was the scoop neck surrounded by delicate lace and beadwork.

She congratulated herself that the dress choice was working. Setting it off with a ruby and diamond necklace she picked up from Paris lended her attire extra spice. Plus, jewelry from the past created mystery. She could claim to have inherited it or sell it later. "I enjoyed the painters that would display in Montmartre. But I really enjoyed listening to the poetry recited in the cafés at night."

"Oh, so you enjoy poetry," he said, starting to sound more interested. Now knowing he was friends with Ezra Pound, she had her hook. If she could work her way into their group as a poet, it would be a lucky break for her.

"Why, yes. I'm no Ezra Pound, of course, but I have dabbled at it now and again." She flushed, knowing that most of the time, her rhymes were horrid. But she figured maybe this would be that common ground for them both.

"Yes, well, as a friend of Ezra's, I've come to know a group of artists, a lot are writers and poets, that meet in London. If you care to listen, I bet they'll top some of those French recitations." His eyes started to light with an inner fire. "In fact, there is talk of starting a new movement to try to put England on the map, so to speak."

"Really?" She perked up at this. She rested her hand on her chin, putting on her mesmerized look. It was her best batting of the eyelashes. After two weeks of scoping out the locals, she finally seemed close to getting an invitation to one of the Vorticists' parties at the Restaurant de la Tour Eiffel.

"Tonight, we're holding our weekly meeting." He smiled with the spark still lit. "In fact, I'd love to have you join me, if you have the time available. We're meeting at a lovely French restaurant," he added with that wink.

She couldn't believe her luck, but tried to appear nonchalant and gracious. "Of course. I always love a good poetry reading."

At precisely eight that evening, a carriage pulled up to the Castle Hotel. John Spencer jumped out with a spring of determination. He entered the hotel to find Deidre sitting in the lobby. She smiled, gliding over to meet him.

"Good evening, Deidre. I've got the carriage waiting. And a small surprise."

She let him take her hand as he guided her toward the lobby door. Holding onto him for balance, she stepped into the black carriage. A man was already seated in the carriage, and she recognized Ezra immediately. He matched one of the portraits she had studied for this mission.

John made the introductions. "Deidre, may I introduce you to Ezra Pound. He was in Hampstead visiting with an associate, and I asked if he would join us for the ride back into the city."

"What a lovely surprise. I'm pleased to meet you, Mr. Pound."

Ezra nodded to her. "Please, call me Ezra. John has been telling me a lot about you. He mentioned you have an interest in poetry."

"Yes, I have been an admirer for years, but haven't seemed to find my style yet." She made a mental note that she might have to come up with some attempted examples. "Maybe you can help me find a direction." She flashed her dimples, hoping it would encourage him to help.

"Yes, my dear. What subject have you tried writing on?"

"Flowers, birds, but most of all, fashion. I adore the feel of a properly fitted dress."

John laughed, adding, "Something I think Deidre is a specialist in."

"Really, my dear John. I didn't think you'd noticed." She added the pout. Hopefully the new black beaded and blue dress she had on would make the poetic fashion statement. Intimate connections would be helpful too. She had chosen the darker color of the hat to accent her hair color. She wiggled her hips. "Fashion is something that never fades in time. In fact, it is fluid like time, changing with the moment."

Ezra perked up with her comment. Good, he could think that she was more than just a pretty face on John's arm. He took up the lead into the subject. "Fashion is something that is, indeed, helped by the new industrial age. With the ability to manufacture cloth, it has led to a revolution in design. More opportunity to produce for the masses."

"Indeed, Mr.— Ezra." She sat up, diving into the debate. "In fact, I would say it has freed up the feminine spirit to pursue something that has always been natural, to create illusion with each new outfit. Before, women could only own a few dresses. Now, a whole wardrobe is essential. In fact, I make it a point to pick up a new dress in every city. I have quite a collection to take home with me to the States."

"I do hope you will happily model these for us," Ezra added. He turned to John. "With the look I've seen coming from John, I would imagine he'd be looking especially forward to seeing you wear the collection from your travels."

Deidre smiled at the last comment. She would have to do an emergency shopping trip to meet the challenge. But it would be worth it. "I'd love to."

The carriage pulled up to the Restaurant de la Tour Eiffel on Percy Street. John held the door for her as she stepped out. Ezra followed behind. They talked to the maître d' like an old friend as he led them toward the back. John indicated to the table where many of his friends had already arrived. If Ezra's association was any indication, this would be the right group of friends, the Vorticists.

She kept a demure look on her face, but gave a little swivel to her step. She wanted to look like an asset to John to gain entrance to this select group. She had what they needed. Money and looks. It was what any artistic movement needed to gain traction. She smiled as she wove around the tables and chairs. Money could buy anything, including research.

A black mustachioed man wearing a half apron approached. He held out a hand to John in welcome. "Mr. Spencer, how good to see you again." He nodded to Ezra. "Mr. Pound. I see you have a very beautiful guest." His French accent reminded her of Montmartre. She was starting to ache for Paris already. "You have brought more patrons to my humble little restaurant, No?"

Ezra answered, "Good evening, Rudolph. We have a budding poet among us. May I present Miss Deidre Thompson from the United States. She's only been in London for a few weeks, but rumor has it her favorite city so far has been Paris," he said with a wink to the proud Frenchman. "We are appreciative that she graces us with her company tonight."

Deidre nodded to Rudolph. He looked more charming than in the famous painting of his restaurant. "I am already missing Paris. Do you have escargot? I haven't had any French cuisine since leaving Paris. I am feeling quite hopeful from John's description of your lovely restaurant."

The glow of pride lit up Rudolph's eyes. "But of course, Miss Thompson. I wanted to bring a little bit of Paris to the English. An enlightenment of the palate, so to speak." He chuckled.

His laugh was infectious. Deidre couldn't help but to smile back. "I so look forward to your menu. By chance, any *guinguet*?"

Rudolph smiled broadly as he nodded. "Why, yes. I will check in my cellar this very moment." He snapped his fingers and a waiter came over. "Select the finest *guinguet* we have for Miss Thompson." The waiter nodded and disappeared. The owner returned his gaze, clapping his hands together, keeping them raised high while wiggling his fingers. "Come, I will show you to your regular table."

He led them to the back of the restaurant. Deidre looked about at the drab mustard-colored walls. They needed to be perked up with some paintings. Then she smiled. The walls were exactly what the Vorticists needed, a place to display. The walls begged for paintings, and she knew from her research that the movement would use the restaurant later as a place to display their paintings, decorating the walls with Vorticist originals. .

A long, rectangular table was set with a white tablecloth. Wooden chairs filled with people surrounding the table. They were all talking and drinking red wine. It was a miniature Montmartre in the making. She was sure she could help spearhead the movement and get much-needed details about the Vorticists' beginnings. So much had been lost when information had been translated from physical copies to digital. She was hoping for a new discovery. It would bring her great recognition in time-travel journals.

A man with wild red hair sat at the far end of the table. A charismatic gentleman sat with a blonde woman, her hair swept into a bun, listening to his every word. A middle-aged fellow sat across the table, nodding to different statements. The conversation stopped as Ezra began the introductions.

"May I present Miss Deidre Thompson, John's new American friend. She is concluding a tour of Europe's greatest cities, and her favorite city so far is Paris. She is a friend of the arts, and John mentioned to me that she might enjoy dinner with our little group so she can tell her friends about us when she returns home."

"Welcome, Deidre." The man who had been the center of the discussion raised his glass. "Anyone who has graced the streets of Paris and decided to venture to London must be shown the greater side of English culture. Civility." Everyone joined him and raised their glasses too.

As she sat, she answered, "Thank you. It's good to feel welcomed. I will be too happy to raise my glass to you as soon as the waiter returns. I am looking forward to a good *guinguet*."

The man that had made the toast stood. "May I introduce myself. I'm Wyndham Lewis. Across from me is Cuthbert Hamilton. This is Helen Saunders." The woman nodded, and Deidre felt the sting of her sharp look. Deidre knew her face was pretty enough to catch the occasional glare from other women. "Over here is Frederick Etchells." He gestured to the man on his left.

With John and Ezra seated on either side of her, it looked like a full table for tonight's dinner. At that moment, the waiter arrived with a small bottle of *guinguet* for her while Wyndham sat down. Grabbing a glass from the other table, he poured some wine while agreeing to get more for the table.

"You've arrived at a rather opportune moment, Ezra," continued Wyndham.

"Oh?" Ezra raised his eyebrow.

"We've been discussing the brilliance of the Expressionists and why England doesn't have its own group of Bohemians."

"And that maybe we should," added Helen in a conspiratorial way.

"We have everything else," he went on. "The industry is here building for the world. Our factories are turning out items that spur our economy. What we need now is something to capture the spirit of the machine age. Something that could go down in time for all to remember."

Deidre was captivated by Wyndham's passion. She could understand now why he was the soul of the Vorticists. It was his passion that underlined the thoughts of the movement. It was breathtaking to watch it happening before her. She sipped some wine, rapt by the discussion.

Ezra interrupted Wyndham. "But if it is to be an artistic movement that England needs, how should it begin?"

Wyndham rapped the table. "By God, it can begin here. In the very bowels of London, from the heart of the empire. We're steaming into the new century with no vision of where we are going. The art that we create now could be that vision. Our work could show how machines and science are changing society and where it can be led."

Deidre took another sip from her glass, and then she saw him. The mysterious man. Through the smoke of the back room, she saw him sitting at a table by the wall. It was the same way he looked at her that night in Montmartre fifteen years ago, only a few weeks in her timeline, and again in Calais at the restaurant by the ferry. His blue eyes were watching her. There was no mistaking his stare. It was definitely the same man.

He raised his glass to her again, and smiled.

Seven

There could be no mistake this time. He was wearing a dark blue suit with matching tie. Although his clothes were different, they were similar to those he'd worn before. His dark hair was cut short, and he had the nightly stubble of evening. His chiseled jaw would make any sculptor jealous. She longed to caress it. To study it.

She took another sip of wine to shake off the spell of rapture he was weaving. If she kept staring at him too long, he would see he'd gotten to her. There was something about him that drew her to him. His gaze was magnetic.

She got a nudge from John beside her. "Deidre, what do you think?"

Deidre pulled her attention back to the conversation. She never let distractions get too out of control. Research was the prime focus. "What? I'm sorry, I was thinking of how good this wine is. What was it?"

"Wyndham asked how your poetry is affected by the Modern Age?"

"Oh." She had to think fast. "Mostly, I think…" She paused to gather her thoughts. What was poetic and machine-like at the same time? "The art of love. It has a beauty but purpose at the same time. The body so driven to reproduce, it will make you believe anything."

"To the body, the ultimate machine," echoed Wyndham. Everyone raised their glasses as Deidre's eyes drifted to the dark-haired man. His spell reached across the room, holding her in place. She longed to feel his chest under his crisp dress shirt. Feel his lips on hers. She was starting to enjoy his eyes beaming his interest from across the room. It was beginning to feel almost too welcoming, even maybe dangerous. She could get lost in that stare.

The haunting eyes of the mysterious man stayed with her. Who was he? Why was he showing up everywhere she went? Why was he in Montmartre, and then fifteen years later, London? He hadn't aged. He looked the same as he did in Montmartre except for a change of clothes. Should she approach him to find out? Or try to stay away? She thought she was going to have trouble keeping her distance. She was starting to imagine what it would be like to kiss him. To feel the softness of his lips, and the lingering feel of his arms around her. He definitely was going to be bad for research.

She looked back to the table where he had been before the toast. He was gone. She took another drink, chastising herself for missing his exit again. He was good at disappearing. She was going to have to solve the mystery about him. There was only one way to do that: talk to him.

First, she was going to have to find him. But how? For now, the mysterious man was going to have to wait. Her first priority was the mission. She first had to find a French fashion designer and dress to impress the Vorticists. Then, she'd solve his mystery. But she knew when she least expected it, she'd see him again.

After dinner, John escorted her back to her hotel. The evening had progressed well. Wyndom had raved about the need to establish their new group immediately. She was invited to join them for a special dinner meeting tomorrow. , excited to not only have found the Vorticists, but that she had found them just at the start of their movement. As they parted, John made her pledge to wear one of the dresses she'd acquired in Paris.

The next day, shopping for a dress for tonight's dinner party was top priority. She needed to impress them, and the dress needed to be fitting of her role as American heiress. To pull it off, she needed a wardrobe that would turn eyes to her. The mysterious man would have to wait. Meanwhile, she would keep her eyes open for him, just in case he chose to show up again.

Deidre headed out in her car after breakfast. She was heading to one of the famed London department stores called Selfridges on Oxford Street. It was still in its infancy since only opening in 1909. She was ecstatic to look at this historical retail shop. It was supposed to be a refuge for the middle-class woman. She wanted to experience it firsthand.

The digital map tracking system found the address, and she set course for it. She looked out the window as she wove through the streets, thinking about what new dresses she'd have made, or maybe find a dress ready to wear. The department-store concept was making it easier for woman to buy things on hand. It would revolutionize this time period.

The Napier arrived at the front drop off of the opulent emporium.. Roman columns and glass structures ornamented the front of the department store, which went on for several blocks. She got out, closing the door, and walked toward the entrance.

"Harry, come back to pick me up in about three hours. Find me then." The hologram inside the vehicle nodded and left the curb to merge into traffic. She looked up at the impressive statue towering over the entrance.

She had to lean so far back to view the statue that she had to hold her hat on so it wouldn't fall off. It was a copper and stone winged angel wearing a flowing lapis lazuli dress. The statue seemed to beg the visitor to enter. She held the world in her hand, gesturing upward at the store. Other ladies in conversation moved past her and entered the store, clearly not as enthralled by the building décor She followed them in, trying not to be overwhelmed by the retail palace.

When she got inside, she couldn't contain the gasp that came out. Opulence was not enough to describe what she saw. Chandeliers hung from a high, ornate ceiling. Velvet-fringed curtains draped the walls. Cases of merchandise spread throughout the whole floor, all lit by new electric lights. She walked past the colognes and perfumes glittering in the glass cases. All looked like jewels waiting for her to pluck.

"May I be of service, miss?" The crisp English accent sounded kind and business-like. A middle-aged woman strode up to her, hands folded in an attentive manner.

"Yes," replied Deidre. "I'd like to have a dress made in the latest French fashion."

"Any particular color, my dear?"

"Red and gold. I'll need it ready in a few days. I'll pay extra."

The woman looked about. "If you wait for a moment, I'll have someone show you the way upstairs to our dresses department." She snapped her fingers, and a dapper gentleman strolled from another aisle and bowed before Deidre. The saleswoman spoke first. "Michael can show you upstairs to our women's department. I'm sure one of our dressmakers can help you up there."

"Follow me, please." He extended a finger curling toward him to follow, turned, and led the way to an elevator bank, where elevator attendants stood at attention, ready to serve. Michael stopped in front of one and gave a brisk order. "Please take this woman to the third floor. She needs to go to the dress department." The uniformed man nodded, and Deidre went into the car. Michael waved back. "I do hope you enjoy your shopping experience with us here at Selfridges."

Deidre nodded as the attendant pulled the metal door shut and moved a lever locking the door. He pushed some buttons, and the elevator began its assent. When the elevator stopped, the attendant announced, "Third floor, ladies' dresses, hats, coats, and undergarments."

She held back a giggle, thinking she'd heard that somewhere in her training. They used to announce things like that. It was amusing to see it in person. She followed the path from the elevator, looking at the merchandise displayed. She saw the hats on individual posts that were arranged at different heights to show off the dimensions of all the hats at once. Mirrors were on square columns throughout the floor. Intricate patterns graced the carpets fit for a mansion. She was walking through a tribute to shopping.

Ahead, she saw mannequins displaying dresses and walked over to take a look at them. Each outfit was matching and in fashion for a middle-class woman of the time. Hats, jackets, and blouses were completely fitted on the mannequin. A woman didn't have to guess, but could buy the whole ensemble.

A nice-looking woman, dressed in a blue suit and scarf with a similar blouse to the woman downstairs approached her. "Good morning, miss. May I interest you in one of these outfits?"

"Actually, I was hoping for something more in vogue. Less the casually dressed woman. I need a fabulous designer gown. Cost is no object. I need the dress by Friday evening and one for tonight. Can you do it?"

The woman looked her up and down. She smiled. "With a figure like yours, I'm sure we will find you something magnificent."

The saleswoman took her aside and had her sit down in a small salon. A dressmaker came to take her measurements. After her fitting, and the order of two dresses, she chose a black beaded silk dress trimmed with black lace that fit her perfectly for tonight's dinner party.

The dressmaker fussed around the edge of the dress, caressing the seams. "Your figure displays the dresses so well, you should be a model, dear. Your figure is perfect."

Deidre just smiled kindly. "Maybe some other time. Thank you. What I really need is a designer dress."

The dressmaker stopped smoothing out the material as Deidre did a pose in the mirror. "There is a French designer who might have a dress in stock form a past show. His name is Paul Poiret. Some of the shops that deal with left over show fashions might have a dress."

Deidre left Selfridges with the assurance she could return in two days for her orders. She also purchased one of the more casual ready-to-wear outfits, a skirt and blouse, which she wore out of the store. She was on the hunt now for an official designer dress.

She programmed in the French designer, Paul Poiret. With a famous designer, she was hoping to impress the artists and show them she could be a backer as well as a member. Having a famous designer available to her might come in handy. But to address her more immediate needs, she hoped to pick up a dress already made in her size. After all, the dressmaker had said she had a perfect figure.

A search of the surrounding shops gave her the location of a dress seller not too far from Oxford Street that had some of Poiret's gowns left over from a show. She was hoping one would fit. She directed the car to head over to the next dress shop. She wanted to get at least something purchased to ensure she'd make a splash at future dinners.

As she headed away from Oxford Street, she noticed the shops beginning to look more deserted and shabby. Cars were less prevalent in this neighborhood. People were walking more on the dirt-lined street. Wagons started to crowd the street, making it hard to pass.

Deidre noticed people staring at her car more often. She leaned back in her seat, looking through the window. Her blonde curls were coming down out of her hat after the extensive fitting.

She'd have to fix that later. She tried to tuck some back under the hat when the Napier pulled up at a shop.

It looked deserted. The peeling paint had the name Mercantile & Fabric, but everything appeared closed. It wasn't the first time that information had been wrong in the digital map database. Some records weren't as thorough as those of other time periods. She opened the door and got out to go to look in the windows.

She pressed up against the front window and leaned in to see in the shop. There was no lighting, and thick dust covered most of the counters. It looked like it had been closed for some time. It was a shame. She was looking forward to wearing a famous designer. It would be a treat to see something in person instead of in a black and white jpeg.

Deidre heard a shuffle behind her and turned. Four men startled her as they walked up. They wore workers' clothes that were filthy and tattered. They were all unshaven, and one was smoking a cigar. He took the cigar from his mouth, exposing brown, rotting teeth, and said, "Beg your pardon, miss, but do you have a 'bob' or two for some down and out folk like us. Been an awful long time since we've had a meal."

She held her purse with both hands and stepped back. "I'm sorry. I don't have any extra change."

"We'll take what we need then."

They came toward her, one grabbing her arm. Another grabbed her purse. Deidre didn't know what happened next. It seemed like a whirlwind of action. A man came from the alley to the side and jumped the man closest to him.

It gave her a chance to do a twist and pull the cigar man's arm back until he begged for mercy. Defensive moves from timeanaut training came back to her. She turned to be ready for the other man, fending off his grab. But the man with the cigar grabbed her again. There was a crack, and the cigar fell out of his mouth as he went down. She turned to see who was helping her. It was him—the familiar stranger.

The mysterious dark-haired man looked focused and alert. She quickly dispatched the man that came at her from behind, sending him spiraling to the dirt. The man ran off quickly as the last attacker was knocked back by the mysterious man. He yelled, "Quick, in the car." She jumped into the open door of her time vehicle, followed by the mysterious man. She yelled to the driver, "Engage." The car sped away, leaving the last attacker standing up and brushing himself off. Another man tried to run after them, but gave up.

She turned to see the mysterious stranger looking at her. He slapped his hands together. "We make a good team."

Deidre tried to straighten her new skirt, which she thought might have a slight tear at the side. It would be a shame if she had ruined this outfit already. "Thank you. They were so fast." She brushed off the dirt from her skirt.

"I'm glad I could help, Deidre."

She stared at him. His eyes were haunting as he started to grin. "How did you know my name?"

"Montmartre had more ripple effects than you might have intended. I was sent to help you. I'm Maxwell Fielding. I've been assigned as your new partner." He held out his hand.

She eyed him carefully. "How do you know the true nature of Montmartre?"

"Did you forget your code word?"

"No."

"Then, this should help. Research is everything."

She hadn't thought she'd need the research help code, but it was such a shock that the stranger was her new assigned partner. Deidre had been working solo on the last two missions. She didn't want to remember what had happened to separate her from James. She didn't want things to go terribly wrong again.

"I think you better tell me everything," she answered.

"I can tell you on the way back to the hotel."

She felt flustered. Licking her lips, her voice sounded unsteady when she spoke. "How do I know you won't compromise my virtue? Back to the hotel please, Harry." The hologram nodded through the window.

"You don't have to keep up your character with me. I know we're in your assigned time vehicle."

The car rolled down the street passing through London. She lifted an eyebrow. "So show me where things may be?"

He hit some buttons on the side, and the control panel dropped for him. Well, the system did recognize his fingerprints. He must have been on other assignments before hers. She looked at him. "Very well. The system recognizes you. But I'm not sure why you're here. You mentioned ripples from Montmartre?"

"Yes. Well, the Council has decided you've been on your own long enough. Since James is gone, I'm to take his place."

She grew upset at this. "Damn it. I can do this on my own. I don't need another partner."

She didn't add that she couldn't go through losing another partner.

"But I have been sent to assist you. It also appears that women traveling alone tend to stick out more in history. In fact, that incident with the men was going to get very ugly had I not stepped in."

She glared at him. "I would have handled them."

"Not the knife. They were planning to kill you. You don't want to know the rest. It was a very public execution for them." Her stare must have given him the hint to continue on. "So, the Time Council decided that it wasn't worth losing the life of an agent. They sent me to save you, and to assist from now on. It's getting too dangerous for you to be on your own."

"That's sexist." She yelled that more than she intended. "I really didn't think I was in danger." She was a little stunned she had almost died. If the timeline was altered by her death, it must have rippled back to the Council's records. The timeline was monitored by people called Watchers to observe time ripples. A ripple must have alerted them.

She'd done some time on that job. In fact, it was required for timeanauts not on duty to monitor the timeline. She had seen the ripples in time happen. Now she realized, she had almost been one of them. Fortunately for her, it wasn't permanent. The Council had stepped in and sent this mysterious stranger. No. He said Maxwell was his name.

He leaned back in the seat. "It's a sexist age. It is for your safety. But I'll need a role. What have you set up so far?"

"I'm an heiress from the States on a European tour. Daddy bought the car. Harry the chauffer here is my traveling companion."

"Well, that's a good start." He folded his arms.

She took off her gloves. "The mission is to become part of the Vorticists' artistic movement. I've also made contact with the

Vorticists. I'm assigned to study the sculptor, Henri Gaudier, as well as the beginning of the movement."

"Well, sounds like I can fit in as"—he took a moment to tap his chin—"your brother. Yes, I'm your brother, just in from the States to help you make the crossing back to New York."

"Great. Guess I've got a new partner." She slumped back in the leather seat. She wasn't sure if it was going to work out for better or for worse. She held back the tears. She wasn't going to let what happened to James ruin the mission now. This time, she almost was killed like James. She was going to have to be more careful. She smiled at Max. At least she knew who he was now, and he was on her side.

Eight

They arrived at the hotel and set the time vehicle to maneuver into the stable out back. Deidre showed Max to the lobby. "We're probably going to need another room."

"Good idea. I hope there is an extra one."

They went to the desk, and Deidre rang the bell. The middle-aged woman appeared. Deidre smiled at her. "Good afternoon, Clara. My brother has just arrived. I was hoping that you had a spare room."

The innkeeper grabbed a key from the boxes. "Yes, we have one down the hall. I'm sorry they're not adjoining, but you're on the same floor." She handed Max the key, flipping the registry book for him to sign. "There you go, Mr. Thompson."

"Thank you." Max signed the name the keeper had kindly dubbed him. "I'm glad to be made so welcome."

Clara flushed a bit. "How long will you be staying?"

"As long as my sister. I'm getting her sorted before returning home. I have to admit, I'm looking forward to some time in London. It's been a while since I've been here."

"Oh, where else have you been before?" asked Clara with a breathless smile.

Deidre snorted as she watched his charm affect Clara. She knew being attractive always helped a timeanaut find a way into places to find research. She'd used it a lot herself. She crossed her arms as he continued to impress the innkeeper.

"Lots of different places." He smiled, leaning on the desk. "Berlin, Rome, Paris, Prague. Our family is well traveled." He finished signing the registry in a flourish of handwriting, something all timeanauts had to study since it died out in the early twenty-first century.

"Any baggage?" asked Clara.

"Some. I'm having it sent from London. It should arrive in a day or two. I always travel light. But I see my sister has been shopping. I'm sure she picked me up some things." He winked at Deidre.

Deidre admired his cover. Like for most timeanauts, new clothes could be bought once you arrived to a new time. It was usually her favorite part. Clara interrupted her thoughts. "Shall I put you down for dinner tonight?"

Deidre answered, "No, thank you. We have other plans for tonight."

"But I'd like to try some of your food here. Better than the French, I'd imagine." He gave Clara another one of his winks. She let out a nervous giggle. He was amazing at flirting. She had to give him credit for his initiative. Interacting with people was the best way to gain information. He was a real professional. Maybe he wasn't going to be a bad partner, after all.

They walked up the stairs to their floor. He walked her to her door, and then turned back toward his room. "I'll see you for dinner in a few hours. Get some rest. I'm sorry for being so mysterious. But I had to let the past roll out according to our records, or I wouldn't have been able to save you."

"I understand." She stood looking into his eyes. The deep blue drew her into them. She was getting lost in his gaze.

"See you tonight." His voice broke the spell as she moved the key into the lock.

"Yes. See you." She turned the key and escaped his gaze. Opening the door to the safety of her room, she stepped inside and locked it behind her. She leaned her back against the door, feeling it protect her from her thoughts. "God help me. He's going to be hard to resist." She shook her head. Deidre didn't want history to repeat itself. She would not make the mistake she had with her last partner. She needed a bath. She gathered her toiletries and went down the hall to wash.

The bath did the trick. She was pleased with the modern Victorian plumbing, making things more comfortable for travelers. But it all still rattled while filling the tub. Feeling clean and refreshed, she realized she was looking forward to dinner with her new partner. The afternoon had been quite unsettling.

She was glad she'd decided to pick up the black beaded dress at Selfridges. The black silk dress fit snugly, gripping her hips in the right places, with an overlay of beads to give notice to her shapely bits. She smiled at her reflection. Her hair was done up under the large black-brimmed hat that she'd bought a week before at a hat store. Feathers and beads curled up and around the brim, making it look like art. She'd have to work the dress for all it was worth. Maybe the right touch of sparkle would offset it. There was a knock at the door.

She checked her hips again to make sure all the beadwork was aligned. Then she grabbed the door. Max stood on the other side, fancied up in black tails and white cravat. Damn, he looked good. She bit her lip.

"Ready to go?" he asked. "Almost." She didn't dare tell him what he looked like. She'd get lost in his eyes again, and who knew where that would lead. She let her mind wander to when she'd have to start charging up the crystal to get it fully ready by her next jump. If Max was the expert timeanaut he portrayed himself to be, he'd be used to that side of time travel. She smiled thinking of what an encounter to charge her crystal would be like with him. Heat warmed her cheeks.

She grabbed her small, black velvet purse from Paris. Most men didn't make her feel this way. Maybe it was because he knew what she was. It made a difference. There was no need to hide anything from him. But she wasn't used to this interest, this growing fascination that started when she'd first seen him in Paris. She turned, trying not to look at him, and headed toward the door.

"Off to see if destiny is on our side." She kept moving forward as he moved behind her.

"Well, the record says it is. Just keep that in mind." He winked at her as he grabbed her hand in a casual hold. A jolt leaped up her arm as he touched her. He squeezed her hand, easing the tension that had built up inside her. Maybe a new partner was the medicine she needed.

They made it to the Restaurant de la Tour Eiffel in time for a drink before dinner. They were taken to the table in the back reserved for the soon-to-be-famous group of artists. Wyndham was seated next to Ezra, and Helen sat across. Deidre ignored another evil-eyed stare from Helen as she took the seat between Ezra and Max. Helen leaned nearer to Wyndham like she was claiming her territory. Deidre could tell from Helen's body language it was a challenge. She looked back to Ezra, who was looking at Max strangely. Deidre needed to establish his cover quickly. John Spencer was notably absent.

"My brother has come to accompany me on the crossing back to the States. Max, these are the wonderful artists I was telling you about."

"Good evening, everyone." Max nodded to the others at the table as Ezra started to relax. Deidre breathed a sigh of relief.

Max smiled at the group. "I'm very glad to join you all. Deidre has been telling me about your talented group."

"And about her poetry." Wyndham declared as an announcement.

Max turned to Deidre. "Poetry, really?"

This got the group's attention as they all stared at Deidre expectantly. She blushed. She realized she'd been so busy trying to get her dresses and wardrobe sorted, she'd forgotten about the poetry. "Well, some poetry. I've tried my hand at it."

"My dear, Europe has changed you." Max broke into a smile. "Father was right. It has made you bloom."

Deidre started to grow redder. "Really, it's not very good."

"How about a line," added Ezra. "We'll be the judge of that." The table looked at Deidre still. She was put on the spot, and Max had not helped. She didn't know where to start, but she had to come up with something, or her cover would be hard to uphold.

All that came to her was Paris, and Henri. She took a deep breath and started.

> *"The heart of freedom,*
> *A fragrant breath,*
> *Paris,*
> *Great with light and power*
> *Helping those to flower*
> *And bloom*
> *To their greatest height*
> *Stories high*
> *Among the clouds*
> *To discover self,*
> *Forever needing*
> *The one power of life*
> *Love."*

The table broke into applause. She'd practiced free verse games with Bertram a few times in the café in the past. It seemed like years ago, rather than days. She missed her group of artists back in Paris.

But this new group, applauding her, seemed to enjoy the poetic free verse. Max looked a bit stunned. That was worth the spot he'd put her in. She would show him she was more than a pretty face. It was something that lots of people in the past—and her present—always underestimated about her.

Wyndham spoke first. "Fine lines, my dear. You'll give Ezra a run for his money." He turned to his side, taking a sip of brandy. "Don't you think, Helen?"

She looked Deidre up and down. "It was good." That was all she said. No blessing from the reigning Vorticist Queen. She was hoping to disarm Deidre. From the expressions on the men's faces, Deidre thought she'd made a good impression. Helen's tactics weren't working.

Deidre smiled demurely, taking the acknowledgment as a compliment and not a challenge. She turned to Max and added to their cover. "What do you think Father will think of my new passion?"

"Better than the old I should imagine, sis."

"And what would have been the old passion?" Wyndham asked expectantly.

"Fashion. I want to be a designer." Deidre blushed. That had just slipped out.

"Oh, do you have any designs now?" Wyndham seemed sparked by her answer.

"Well, not sketched. It's sort of like my poetry, spontaneous."

"She is going to fit in well," added Ezra with a smile.

Wyndham nodded, turning to Max. "And, dear sir, what is your line of work?"

"Exploring, mostly. It would be nice to see if I can get some factory started up north. It's what I came to England to do, representing my father's company. Picking up Deidre is a side trip."

Wyndham said, "I'm sure John can help you with that. He has a factory up north as well. Maybe he can help you find the right property."

At that point, she felt the power of wealth switch from her purse to Max's. He had shifted the power of persuasion to himself and hammered the nail in her coffin of finance further by saying, "She was always the creative one. I was always trained for business."

"And a very talented woman for some lucky man." Wyndham saluted Deidre with his glass. Helen started to fume, but he seemingly didn't notice. The waiter appeared, asking for everyone's order. She started to feel smaller and smaller at the table.

Max was definitely putting a spin on this assignment. She felt the interest of conversation turning to him, with some spirited talk directed toward her in good faith to keep her interested. It wasn't that she was dismissed, but had been acknowledged as a follower to the plan of good fortune the men were plotting. Deidre really started to miss Paris.

"Why did you do that?" She was viciously whispering at Max in the hall by their rooms. She'd given him the silent treatment in the taxicab back to the hotel.

"Do what?"

"Embarrass me like that?"

"What was there to be embarrassed about?"

She turned, balled her hands into fists, and released them throwing her hands up in the air. "Have the great heir show up.

It was obvious from the conversation switch that I was now your charge." She waved her hands about her. Disbelief tinged her voice. "They won't talk to me now except to pamper my whims for poetry."

He grabbed her flailing arms, easing them down and holding her shoulders. "Oh, Deidre, I doubt many men can ignore you. Besides, all of it is for your safety. It was becoming unsafe as you traveled forward. Someone had to come be an escort. It was just too dangerous by yourself."

"This is why I hate working with a partner. Men always get the advantage of everything in the past. Women are so secondary."

"This bothers you so?"

He was holding her closer as they spoke. Her attraction to him was getting stronger, magnetic, pulling her closer to him. They were noses apart. The silence grew between them before Deidre answered.

"Yes." She let the pout start. Deidre hoped it worked to get him to suffer for the injustice he'd caused to her research. "It's going to make it harder to do research and get close to them."

"You might have to try other tactics than you've tried before. What about Helen? You can try to get close to her."

She folded her arms. "She is already not happy with me being in the group. I could tell she has a thing for Wyndham."

"You weren't thinking of him as your next subject of study?"

She lowered her hands to her sides as he stood in front of her. "No, I'm assigned the sculptor. But you being here is going to present a problem."

"How so?" He put his arm up against the wall.

He was now pressed against her, his body wedging her against the door, and the urge to be with him was making her concentration sketchy.

She tried to look down. "You tend to be very distracting."

"Were there problems with charging the energy band? How did you manage before?"

She looked up at him. His lips were lingering near hers. He was dangling the facts in front of Deidre. It was not hard to imagine charging the crystal with him. "I had my ways."

She felt his breath over her lips. "They might be similar to mine." He pressed his lips to hers, loosing her hold of resistance, pulling on her lips gently. Slowly, he let her lower lip go. She kept herself standing, barely.

He looked her square in the eye. "If you want to be in charge, I can let you. I'm guessing that is what you like. Or we can be together in other ways to support each other. We will have to charge our crystals sometime."

She swallowed, keeping her sanity as his masculine scent started to make her mind drift to more intimate ways to settle the dispute. "We are brother and sister. It might look out of character to be together."

"Then, later, more private perhaps?" She felt her eyebrow go up.

He drew away, the essence of his heat still lingering. "I bid you a good night, dear sister. Until tomorrow."

She stared after him as he went down the hall and turned the corner. She escaped into her room again and leaned up against the closed door. Yes. She'd rather be working solo. He was too distracting to research. Knowing this, her heart tried to hide the evidence of what her mind was fighting. She couldn't let herself fall for Max. She couldn't fall for another partner. It was too dangerous for the mission and her heart.

Nine

At breakfast he sat across from her, talking made-up small talk about home to help with their covers. She nodded, adding questions to give depth to their ruse. But at the same time, it was getting hard not to imagine their relationship being very different. She kept thinking of that kiss last night, his lips lingering and pulling on hers.

"Deidre, are you listening?" Max interrupted her thoughts.

"Oh, yes."

"Or did you not want to know about your horse back home?"

She brought her mind back to the conversation. "Is he doing well?"

"Yes. He won the last race. Uncle Arnold said he'll be another champion like his father."

She could feel the elephant ears of the patrons around her growing larger at some of their conversation. Little subtle looks her way as her eyes swept the room told her their conversation was working to establish their roles.

Clara came over to their table. "How are my favorite sister and brother? Faring well?"

Deidre answered, "Yes, Clara. I've truly come to enjoy starting my day here each morning. Your breakfasts are delicious. Your English hospitality has surpassed that of Paris."

Max made a face. "Anything is better than being in France."

Deidre waved at him. "Oh, stop that, Max. I still love Paris, no matter how you feel about the French."

Clara was hanging on his every word. "I'm glad you think so, Mr. Thompson." Her eyes grew wide as she continued to speak. "I do wish to go to America someday myself. I hope all Americans are as lovely as you."

"They are, of course." She had to prod Max. "At least, a lot of men think they are as dashing as my dear brother. He really is, however."

"Something only a sister could say." He eyed Deidre knowingly.

Clara laughed and said, "I'll leave you both to your breakfast. If you should need anything, please let me know."

Deidre wiped her mouth with her napkin and kicked Max under the table.

He snapped back, "Hey, what was that for?"

She lowered her napkin. "For being so cozy with Clara."

"You know I can't kick you back. Besides, I'm building connections. We need those."

"Fine. But at least there are some things that only women can do in this century and get away with."

"There are a few more. And we may have to use them full tilt." He lowered his voice. "Shall we go get your dresses sorted?

This time, stay near me. We don't want you wandering into any areas that can get you killed."

They got up from the table, a plan in hand, and went to get the time vehicle out of the stable.

"Max, have you noticed the pair of men behind us?"

He was carrying the carefully wrapped package of Deidre's purchases: tailored dresses, a suit and dress shirt for Max, shoes, and one hatbox. He didn't even break a stride as he answered, "Yes. They've been tailing us since we left the department store."

After leaving Selfridges & Co., they had been walking along Oxford Street for a few blocks when the men following behind them became noticeable. The street was bustling with people making their way here and there. It was the ebb and flow that made these men stand out. They neither ebbed nor flowed, staying close on their heels.

"Any plan?" She didn't move her head. Looking forward, she suggested, "I could have our chauffeur pick us up at the end of the block."

"Do it. I think they mean business."

She hit the emergency pickup jewel on her bracelet. It looked like she fiddled with it for a second. This slowed their walking pace so she could see what the men behind them would do. The men slowed and matched their pace.

"Don't look behind again. I think they may have seen you, Deidre." He put his hand protectively behind her waist.

"If they know, they'll break off the chase."

He nodded forward. "Not necessarily. They might take it up a notch."

He was right. The men sped up. One man grabbed Deidre's arm as the other reached for Max. "Now, let's not have any funny business." The man twisted Deidre's arm as he spoke. "You two are coming with us." He spoke to them with a thick cockney accent that was very out of place in the shopping district.

"No, sir. We won't be going anywhere with you." Max stopped moving.

"Come on, gov'na', don't make us hurt ya kind sister." He spit out the last word, grabbing Deidre's arm.

"Who sent you?" She tried to wring out of his grip, but he had her too tightly. "If you don't let us go, I'll scream."

Her comment made the man grip her more tightly. "Come with us, Deidre." He dropped his cockney accent. "You're not supposed to be here now. It will be easier if you just come along." She stomped on his foot with her heel, distracting the man, and gave Max a chance to break free from his attacker. As her attacker was getting back up, she caught him off guard and slammed her elbow into the side of his head. He went down. She saw Max make a similar move on his man, but not enough to take him out. The time vehicle was at the corner, and they simultaneously saw it and made a run for it. Deidre grabbed her dress package on the way, but in her haste, the hat and suit was left behind.

As Max and Deidre approached the time vehicle, they could hear rapid footfalls behind them. Max got to the door and opened it, just as his attacker grabbed Deidre. She turned and flung the dress bag toward his face with one hand and landed an upper cut with the other, taking him off balance. Max punched him in the jaw, and dropped him to the ground. They both climbed into the car, leaving the attacker by the curb.

"What was that?" she yelled as she felt the vehicle rumble into motion.

"Some of London's finest. Failed in their attempt to rob us, I imagine. They weren't ready for you to fight back." He was smiling, almost into a chuckle.

"I don't know. They seemed to want to take us somewhere. We gave them a surprise." He began laughing. "Why are you laughing? I have basic defense training."

"Well, that's not what I'm laughing about. The fact that you grabbed the dresses shows your priorities."

"I do need to wear something. I'm just sad you dropped the hat and your suit."

He turned to the materializer and connected his wristband to it. The lost hat appeared in 3D-form, ready to wear on the tray. "I did manage to take a visual 3D capture of it for research. It won't feel the same as real wool, but it will do. My suit will be harder to replicate. But I'll get another."

"What more could a woman want?" She had to laugh at his quick thinking. But in the end, she couldn't help but wonder what the men were after. Was it really a robbery? Or something more sinister? It was strange to be attacked twice in just two days. Was it all just bad luck, or something else she couldn't put her finger on? She pondered what to do next as they returned to the hotel.

Max sat across from her not saying a word. If he had thoughts on the matter, he didn't say anything the rest of the trip. But it still was strange. A new partner, two attacks, all so close to each other. They had to be connected in some way.

They made it back to the hotel and dressed for dinner. They had another dinner engagement planned with the Vorticists. Deidre wanted to wear the burgundy and cream silk dress she had saved from the attack. Max met her at her room.

"You are a vision, Deidre." Max moved closer to her, his breath whispering near her cheeks.

"You're not acting like my brother right now."

"I'm not feeling like your brother." He grabbed her waist, feeling the contours of the dress. "We could be a little late for dinner. I am, after all, your new partner."

She placed her finger on his lips. "It's too soon, Max. I've only been with men when I needed them. But I think we need to keep things professional for now. Besides, you still need to pretend to be my brother." He moved back as she smoothed her dress, trying to ignore how fast her heart was beating from his touch. "Best we be getting to dinner. We'll never get through the traffic unless we leave now."

He let her go. "I'm sorry. It's just that I was so attracted to you back when we were in training… I'd hoped we'd be able to work together some day, and when I got this assignment, I thought…"

She looked up, recognizing him a little now. "Wait. I think I do remember you in some of my classes. But you were always near the back, quiet and shy."

"Yes. But some of my assignments have changed me. The past can do that." The twinkle in his eye made him quite attractive. She let the thought linger for a moment, and then put her hand on his shoulder. "You're right. The past can change you. So let's give the past some time to have its effect on us. Back to the mission. We have a dinner to attend."

He put out his arm, and she hooked hers in his. "As a very caring brother, it's my duty to look out for you. For now."

"And how else later?" She looked up at him with a smirk.

"Maybe time will tell. Maybe you'll grow to love me as more than a brother."

The restaurant was packed. Smoke filled the parlor and created a fog around the Vorticists, making them appear almost ethereal, holding court on the ways of art. Deidre had managed to escape another poetry reading so far. She was feeling very relaxed from the wine and chatter.

Cuthbert Hamilton was noticeably absent tonight. Ezra Pound was quite vocal in his arguments of what the movement should be. But John Spencer was here, seemingly delayed for business from the last dinner. John Spencer watched the people around him, his eyes aglitter with the high that brushing arms with artists evoked.

She was intrigued with the artistic excitement she was watching unfold before her. This was the rush she got from her research. She looked over at Ezra as she took a sip of wine. He was very attractive when arguing his opinion.

Wyndham waved at Ezra. "I can see your point. But I want to talk about what we've worked out so far. If you'll let me."

"Go right ahead, then. You've got your pigheaded mind set to it." Ezra folded his arms. She knew that the argument was leaning in Wyndham's favor.

Wyndham stood up. He raised his glass to begin. "I'd like to officially declare the start of a new artistic movement. Someday, this very spot will be famous for this moment."

The hairs on the back of Deidre's neck stood up as he continued. She tried not to look over at Max. Wyndham couldn't know how true his words were as he continued. "I declare the start of a new age. One in which art is viewed through the very lens of technology and innovation. The machinist point of view is born. I have a manifesto that I have been working on that will be in the first magazine of the movement. I want you all to contribute. I welcome your insight, even yours, Ezra." He held up his glass toward Ezra.

Ezra nodded. "You always gloat when you win. If you want to take all the credit for the manifesto, fine. But at least my ideas will live on within it."

Wyndham went on. "As so they should, my friend. We are all in this together." He raised his glass as everyone sounded out a "Here, here" or "Hurrah."

"Then, it's settled. We begin plans for the Vorticists' first magazine." He drank and put the glass down. "John has given us permission to hold our first meeting at his estate. Which means, everyone, I'm assigning a bit of homework to all of you." He clasped his hands together, then took a moment to look at each person as he spoke. "You must bring a contribution worthy of the first edition for our new magazine to John's at our next meeting. And there will be no exceptions." He turned to Deidre with a warm smile. "Except maybe Deidre, since she is so shy about her poetry."

She felt the warmth spreading across her face. Though Wyndham had given her an out, she knew she was going to have to write something. She knew it would be the first of only two editions to mark the movement. Whether her piece made it into the magazine wasn't important. She had to look like she was trying to be part of the group.

She did remember the *Blast* cover and edition she'd seen during research in the time vehicle. It didn't mention her name in it. She wasn't sure what to make of that, especially since she had nodded, agreeing to bring a poem to this meeting. She shook her head. It must not have been up to their standards and they didn't include it. That had to be why it wasn't listed in the research. But she wished that she could write something that would gain their praise.

She was brought back to the moment by Wyndham's toast. "To the Vorticists, may we bring an enlightened look into the hearts of the English and civility to the understanding in this new age of machinery." They all held their glasses aloft.

She looked over to Max. His eyes seized hers. Deidre raised her glass to him. "To making history."

He raised his glass to her. "To making history."

He was looking at her not as a brother at all. She nodded back, smiling.

She held an ink pen over the paper. The page stood blank before her. She couldn't write a single word. She had to get something on paper, and it had to be staggering in the effort to impress. She dipped the tip in ink again, thinking that this would bring forth her first words. Staring at the stationery she wrote a title: "Love." It was all she could think of at the moment.

She needed to get some words written before going to bed. She knew she wouldn't be able to get to sleep until she had started it. But nothing was coming to her.

There was a knock. It broke her concentration. She put the pen back in the well and headed to the door. It was Max. He was grinning from ear to ear. "What are you doing now?"

She returned his smile. "Writing a poem. I'm trying to become that poetess they are expecting. Are you here to offer some help?"

"Well, I can try to help if you let me in."

She stepped aside as he came into the room. She shut the door and watched him sit on the side of her bed. "What are you having trouble with?"

"Just getting started." She sat next to him.

"What do you have so far?" He leaned over to see the paper she was holding.

She held it up for him to see. "The title. Love."

"Well, it's something."

"If you were writing a poem about love, how would it go?"

He tapped his chin. "I think I'd take some time to be alone to think about it. At least a day."

"And?" She felt him turn to look at her.

He leaned near. "I would write the poem to someone specific."

"Someone you love?"

"Yes. I would let myself explore the feelings I had about her." He whispered in her ear. "I'd open up completely and let the words spill onto the page"—his breath caressed her cheek—"each one carefully chosen to reflect my true feelings."

He moved his lips closer to hers and slipped his arm behind her on the bed. She felt the warmth of his body. "I'd let her know, word by word, line by line, what it meant to be with her"—his leg touched her thigh—"building up to the climax in which I'd profess my undying love." He reached toward her face and slipped a stray lock of hair behind her ear. "If I were writing a poem on love, that's what I would want to say."

"She would be a lucky woman." Deidre swallowed, her heart beating faster in her chest. His eyes drew her in. "But that still leaves me with a blank page. How do I start?"

He looked her directly in the eyes. "Write the poem to someone you love, Deidre."

"What if I'm not sure if I've ever been in love?"

"You've never been in love?"

"I think I have." She thought about James. How she felt torn with the loss of him. "The sense of loss I felt after losing someone I cared about had to mean I'd been in love, right?"

"You'd know." He broke the eye contact and got up. "I'll leave you to your writing." He stood up and started toward the door.

"You could stay a bit longer and help, Max." Her voice held the loneliness she'd been feeling through the last two time-jumps. "Maybe I do need a partner in this. In everything."

He looked at her. "I'm glad you're seeing it that way. It must have been hard for you to lose James. Timeanaut partners can get very close."

She looked down. "We were."

Her answer seemed to startle him. "I'm not surprised. James was a good-looking man."

"It wasn't just that." She looked at Max. "We had each other's backs too."

"And probably charged your bracelets together."

She nodded slowly. "You've been with other partners before. You know how it is."

"Yes, but sometimes, you meet that someone special, and there is no one else." He turned suddenly and opened the door. "Good night, Deidre."

Her "good night" bounced off the closing door. She could hear his footsteps thumping down the hall. The hollowness echoed in her heart. She looked at the blank paper in her lap. Love. Who would she write her poem to? She got up and moved to the desk, feeling that she needed to write to two different people. Two poems. She smiled as she dipped the pen in ink and began her first line.

Ten

John Spencer's estate was outside of London near a village named Great Missenden in Buckinghamshire. Along the railway route, it was a main thoroughfare for the early commuting population of London to live, write, and create art, and still have access to the capital. It was also a place to get away from the bustle of business, as the Vorticists called it. An encampment in which to think and create a movement, with access to the modern marvels it so wanted to illuminate. Deidre loved it immediately.

She stepped off the train to see a Victorian station at its peak, recently built, in pristine order. She loved traveling when she could note all of the buildings lost to time. They became part of her report. So much is lost by the destruction of generations. She looked about the small terminal, and Max followed behind. He called over a porter to help with their bags.

She turned to Max. "Could you see about getting us a taxi? We'll need one to take us out to the estate."

"Right. Let me get us sorted first." Max placed a coin into the porter's hand. "You heard the lady. We need a taxi to take us to the Spencer Estate."

The porter nodded and added, "You may have to hire a carriage, sir. There is a stable to hire someone nearby." He started loading their trunks onto a large cart.

Max held Deidre by the arm. "Sister dear, do you want to take some time to rest before heading out? Maybe a cup of tea?"

The porter interrupted, "There is a lovely tea shop in town down the hill."

Deidre smiled at him. "That actually sounds wonderful. It would be nice to take a break before heading out on the last leg of the trip."

Max nudged her on her back with his hand. "I'll make the arrangements and meet you in the tea shop."

Max caught up to the porter with determination in his stride. She was starting to get used to him taking charge. Her worries definitely were halved now that he was with her. They were making a good team.

She walked to the shop, enjoying the swish of her skirts as the new petticoat rustled under her specially designed dress. She had informed the seamstress of some of her ideas that might impress her new artist friends. Or at least she wanted it to look that way. Since she'd declared to them all that fashion had always been an art form she loved, she wanted them to see it was something she was actually good at.

The dress was a deep, rich blue silk, highlighted with burgundy. The colors complemented her hair, as well as her skin tone. She concluded she must look stunning, based on the stares she was getting in the town. Her sweeping, large, black-felt hat spoke of the hat fashion of the time. The ribbon around its brim matched the dress.

Moments after she entered the tea shop and selected a table by the window, the waitress came over to take her order. Deidre asked for tea with cream and sugar. She had been left to wait for its preparation when she felt a tap on her shoulder.

"Pardon me, miss. I think you dropped this." A man stood behind her holding a lace handkerchief.

She gave him one of her warm smiles. He was most likely a pickpocket wanting to trap her. This would be interesting for research. "I'm sorry, sir. I don't own a handkerchief like that."

She started to turn around when he spoke again. "No, I saw you drop it, miss. I assure you, I'm only trying to be polite."

Deidre gave a smirk. "I'm sorry, sir. If this is some kind of game, I would appreciate skipping to the end. It is not mine. So, good day to you."

He grew more desperate in his tone. "Madam, I do believe it is meant for you." He held it out. "Please, take it."

She eyed him, not sure of his motives, but took the handkerchief so as not to cause a scene. "Thank you, then." That's when she felt something held within the kerchief. "I didn't catch your name."

"You won't need it, miss." He tipped his hat. "If you'll excuse me."

"Here's your tea, miss." Deidre turned to receive her drink from the waitress, and when she looked back, the man was gone. She took her tea and sipped it. The handkerchief lay on the table. She couldn't help but wonder what was inside.

She took the bundle in her hand and something fell out onto the table. It was a silver locket with initials on the back that read

J.D. Opening it, there was a picture. She hadn't seen an image of him in the past. It was shocking. The picture was of the man she had loved, her former partner James.

"Is the tea good?" Max's voice caused her to look up.

The shock of Max's appearance made her keep her hand closed over the locket. Her past hidden from the present. "Yes. This is a nice little tea shop for such a small village."

"I'm glad you're comfortable. Looks like we'll have to wait a bit before going out to the estate. I've tried to find someone to drive us out, but it seems there is only one person available to do it. He'll be back in about an hour. Meanwhile, we can wait. After all, you needed a break."

"Yes." Numbness had gone down the length of her body. The black and white tintype in the locket reminded her of his rugged looks, floppy blond hair, and steel-blue eyes. He was brought back in an instant by the photo. James. Her James.

"Deidre?" Max sat on the other side of the table. Concern covered his face.

"What? I was drifting. Sorry." She pulled her hand into her lap, hiding the locket from view.

"Did you ever finish that poem? We'll need something to impress them. Or to make it look like you tried."

The waitress arrived with a cup of tea for Max, and she started to ease out of her fog. "Yes. Of course. I think it is in one of the trunks. I wrote lines about what love means to me."

Max gave her an earnest look. "And what does love mean to you, Deidre?"

"Pain, I think. And confusion."

He took a sip at her comment. She didn't blame James for getting himself killed. The pain was more than she had ever felt.

The locket burned in her hand with no real heat. Just the longing to be held by the man in the photo again. She'd forgotten how much it had hurt. "Longing. That's another line. Love does that."

"Yes, well." Max took another sip. He didn't have to pretend to be awkward like an Englishman when it came to feelings. He was seemingly playing the role to the hilt, or was he truly feeling awkward talking about love? He certainly hadn't had any trouble the night before when he was explaining how he would write a poem about love. She had found his words—and his proximity—intoxicating.

"Is that awkward for you? That word. Love." She wanted to know which it was. Was he feigning his discomfort or was he really not used to love? "Or is it awkward for you to listen to me talk about my past loves?"

His body language told her much. Max couldn't look her in the face. His voice sounded unsteady. "How do you really know when to talk to that someone about it?"

She held the locket tighter. "That's where the confusion comes in. And you should just tell them. Be forward about it."

He still couldn't seem to look at her. She couldn't resist. "Max, have you been in love?"

When he didn't answer, she had to prod him. "Does that mean you haven't? You seemed to speak with a voice of experience last night."

He looked up at her slowly. That's when she knew he must have known love at some point. You didn't look like that unless you had been in love. He answered with two words. "Love hurts."

She grabbed his hand. "Then you agree. It's a dreadful topic to write about if it leaves all this pain."

"No. It is the most wonderful topic of all. It is painful because it's so powerful. I think it's a good topic for your poem. Read it to me later. Maybe I can give you some tips before you present it to the others."

He wiped his mouth, looking anxious to leave. He seemed to be restless, moving around in his chair. "Let's get some air. Maybe this town has a square. We can make it back in fifteen minutes for the carriage, surely."

"Yes. I'm feeling a bit dreary. Maybe it was because of all that time cooped up on the train."

He stood and offered Deidre his hand.

She smiled and reached out her hand without thinking. She was still holding the locket.

"What is that?"

"Oh, it's a family heirloom ," she said, trying to think fast. "I thought I'd put it on today, for old times sake."

"Here. Let me help."

She turned and lifted her hair. He brushed the nape of her neck putting it on, sending shivers through her. She heard his whisper behind her ear, his breath brushing her skin. "Looks like it was made for you."

"Indeed." She had an awkward smile, and touched the locket where it sat on her chest. "It does seem a custom fit."

They took a stroll along the main street of the village, and looked down a side street leading to a residential area. Hedges lined the yards, with wrought iron fences delineating the territory of each home.

"What do you think of this town?" Deidre asked.

"I think it's beautiful." Max stopped in front of a pub on the corner and looked behind him. He seemed distracted.

She looked at him strangely, not understanding why they stopped. "Do you need a pint?"

He silently nodded and directed her inside. He turned around as a man with a bowler followed them in. "Don't turn to look at him. But a man who has been following us just came in through the door."

"How do you know?" she whispered back.

"See. He is heading straight to the bar, but looking around him. He's scanning the place."

"Lots of people come to the local pub looking for someone. He's probably a local at lunch." She dismissed the thought with a wave of her gloved hand as she sat down at a table.

"Deidre, haven't you thought it strange that we've had two groups of men try to jump and rob us? And now this brute is on our trail."

"You're paranoid, Max."

"Am I? Well, if we get up to leave, and he follows us out, then we'll see if I'm paranoid." He got up and headed for the door, knowing she'd have to follow.

She did just that, scampering as her skirt rustled behind her. Max opened the door for her, and she proceeded out. Deidre watched Max turn back to notice the man in the bowler was leaving the pub too.

Max grabbed Deidre by the elbow. "Come on. He's leaving too." He pulled her along as the bowler-topped man followed, offering no pretense to cover his intentions. He kept up with their brisk pace. There was no doubt they were being followed.

Max said, "Doesn't this seem like a lot of coincidences, Deidre? That man back there. I'm sure he means no good."

"Why don't you ask him? Maybe he's just lost."

"I don't want to find out, do you?"

"Actually, yes." She stopped and turned to walk toward the man. Max gasped when he realized she was walking right up to him.

Deidre commanded, "Are you following us, sir?"

Max caught up to Deidre's side and put his arm around her protectively. It was something an older brother would do, and Deidre felt protected.

The man in the bowler looked stunned. "Well yes, miss. I am. You two are from the States, correct?"

Max answered the man first before Deidre could. "Yes. Do you have any business with my sister and I?"

"You are?"

Max stammered. "If you don't even know our names, then why are you following us? What business could you possibly have with two strangers?"

"Let me introduce myself then. Donald is my name. Detective Donald Bradley of the London Police. We are on the alert for a pair of rogues traveling in the area, stealing from our good citizens. We had a report that they might be passing through this village. And since you are clearly new to town, just arrived on the train, I thought I'd keep my eye on you."

Deidre grew wide-eyed. "I hope they aren't here now. We only lingered in the village while we waited for a carriage to get our things out to the Spencer Estate. We will be staying there for the weekend."

"Ah, guests of Mr. Spencer. I see."

Max added, "We're here to meet with artists that he has invited to his estate. I am Max Thompson. This is my sister, Deidre. We have identification if that's what you need."

Max took out his passport to show the detective. He looked it over.

Deidre spoke up. "Will you need to see mine too?" Deidre knew they could always have papers made for them in the time vehicle to help them in their assigned periods. Her identity papers were in her purse.

"No, that will be fine. Your brother's seems in order." He handed the passport back to Max. "I'm just trying to keep tabs on everyone entering the village. Please give my regards to Mr. Spencer."

Max put his passport back into his jacket pocket. "We understand, Detective. You are just doing your job."

The detective tipped his hat and continued to walk down the street past them. They watched him walk for a bit until Deidre said, "That is strange. I didn't know the London police would venture out of the city."

"Not often. Only if they have good reason. It is unusual to see a detective in a small village like this." He checked his watch. "The carriage should be ready now. Shall we go?"

"Odd that he didn't mention where he got the report." Deidre kept looking after the detective.

"Well, I guess we don't really need to know. But there are some strange occurrences happening to us. I suggest we keep our eyes open for more confrontations. Maybe travelers don't stop in this village often."

"No, on the digital map, it said it was a Victorian destination for Londoners to get away. It's just all odd." She started walking to the station and the stables. "First the louts by the dress shop when you helped me. Then, the ones by the department store.

Now, this detective. It feels as if someone is trying to stop or deter us from something."

Max nodded. "Or distract."

"I'm not sure what it all means, but there is something unusual about all this unwanted attention."

Max just nodded. It seemed like he wanted to say more, but turned instead. She followed him down the street to reach the carriage scheduled to take them to the estate.

Eleven

The carriage rolled up the long gravel driveway with a manicured lawn sweeping down before it. Georgian windows outlined by red bricks dotted the tan stone walls. Ivy tangled its way up the walls and around the windows. Soaring chimneys popped up along the stone-railed roof. Manicured hedges lined the paths leading to the main entrance. Red brick created a sweeping column of archways to welcome visitors at the entrance.

It was everything Deidre had imagined an English estate would look like. She grabbed Max's hand tightly, giddy with excitement. "Doesn't it look fabulous?"

Max peeked out the window of the carriage. "It looks very nice."

"It looks so picturesque and beautiful."

"You sound like you'd like to move in and start nesting."

"But it's lovely. It's so nice to be in a personal residence for a change. Inns and hotels don't feed your soul like a real home does."

"Well, a real country manor is a lovely place to feel right at home, Deidre. But don't make yourself too at home. Our host might take it wrong."

She hit him on the shoulder. "You are horrible to tease me this way."

"What else is a brother for?"

She smiled at the way they fit easily into their roles. The show they were putting on for the carriage driver should travel to the gossiping mouths that would ask questions about them in the village. Strangers were always gossip subjects in small villages such as these.

As they rode up the gravel drive, Deidre could smell the hint of lavender from the hedged garden welcoming her to the country. She had the urge to explore the pathways she could see from her window. She wanted to let her feet explore what could be behind the gate hidden mostly by a wall of ivy. The driver took them to the front of the house where a butler and other staff were filing out of the house to greet them.

When the carriage came to a stop, a doorman stepped forward and opened the carriage door for them. "Welcome to East Camptonshire Place. May I have your names to check our guest list."

They slid out of the carriage, and Deidre answered the doorman as Max settled the fare. "It is Mr. and Miss Thompson."

"Very good, miss. Mr. Spencer has asked me to extend his greetings and to escort you to the salon upon your arrival. We'll be sure to place your luggage in your rooms." The doorman snapped his fingers, and two young boys came forward to help the driver unload their trunks. He turned to another young boy who seemed to be around fourteen. "Show Mr. and Miss

Thompson to the east wing salon. They are expected for drinks before dinner."

The young man nodded and turned to them. "If you could follow me, I'll show you inside." He swept his hand toward the marble stairs. Deidre waited for Max to join her. He offered her his arm, and they walked slowly up the steps, Deidre trying not to look too overwhelmed.

"It is so beautiful here." She was at a loss for words. Another man waiting atop the stairs opened the massive front door.

The entire presentation spoke of wealth and prestige. She was impressed that the Vorticists had this much support for their humble beginnings. Rarely had she seen artistic movements without large sums of money supporting them. Those were probably the ones that never survived through history and would be hard to find or research.

After the doorman opened the large wooden doors, the young man took the lead to show them to the salon. She walked through corridors with dark wooden floors and carved wooden ceilings, with ornately framed oil paintings hung along the walls. Dim sunlight illuminated the rooms as she passed. It was opulent even for the Edwardian Age. She loved every minute of her visit so far.

Max followed behind, his umbrella tucked under his arm like any Englishman. He was critically noting the décor, as evident from his furrowed brow. He most likely had the same implant in his brain that she did to store the visual data. But the mental notes she took would be helpful to sort through the cryptic data collected. Smells, feelings, and sensations were still noticed by the human brain. Her interpretations were crucial. She did so love this part of her job.

They arrived at the salon and were greeted by some of the other Vorticists who had already arrived. Mixed in were a few new faces. One man in particular was very attractive. He had wavy brown hair slicked back in the style of the day. His high forehead was creased in worry as he stared into his brandy sifter. His long English nose made him look distinguished, and his thin lips were pursed in worry. She immediately felt drawn to him. Her eyes were locked to him when she heard a familiar voice coming toward her.

"My dear, Deidre." She turned around to see Ezra Pound coming to greet her. He kissed each of her cheeks and continued. "So glad you could make it with your brother. I see he is in tow as ever."

Max didn't miss a beat with him. "I have to keep her in check, Ezra."

"As well you should, Max. She is a flower that must be awoken with the passion of poetry. I'm so looking forward to hearing your work, Deidre dear."

Deidre smiled, grabbing his hand that was waving about before her. "I look forward to how it will be received. I am hoping you all will be gentle. This is my first time sharing my poetry in public."

"In public, my dear? Why, no. You are among friends." Ezra grabbed her other hand and held them. "We will listen and help bring your work to fruition. In fact, let us all have a drink to toast the start of a fulfilling weekend. We should get a lot of work done in the sharing of our contributions for the movement."

"The power that which we can do together will have no measure." It was Wyndham Lewis coming to join them from another room with a drink in hand. "I see you have arrived to contribute to our little soirée, Deidre. I am glad you are able to join us. In fact, there are some of us you haven't had the pleasure to meet yet. Let me introduce you."

Wyndham gently wrapped his arm behind Deidre's waist, gathering her at his side to escort her around the room. Max was left in the company of Ezra, who promptly helped him get a drink. Wyndham introduced Deidre to a group of people by the fireplace—the brooding good-looking man eyed her over his brandy, and two other men stood with him.

Wyndham pointed to each man as he spoke. "Over here we have two of our painters and a sculptor. Edward Wadsworth, a portrait painter, has joined us." A balding middle-aged man with a thin mustache nodded a greeting to her. She nodded back.

Wyndham continued. "Mr. William Roberts, also a portrait painter." Mr. Roberts bowed to her. Wyndham then pointed to the brooding man. "And Henri Gaudier, our young upstart sculptor. Lately, he's been experimenting with Asian imagery and styles."

She looked at the handsome man she'd been eyeing. He was the sculptor she was assigned to study. Deidre made sure she gave him her most winning smile.

Wyndham continued. "Though, I'm not sure how his studies will reflect English ideals."

"Nonsense, Wyndham." Henri seemed to come alive with the taunt. His voice held conviction and depth. "Studying primitive style will get us back to our roots of expression. Leaving an impression is what is important in this age. Simplistic movement is essential to show the inner workings of the human experience."

Wyndham waved his drink. "But is it not best to show the human experience in the English way?"

"Please, the both of you. Save the argument for after dinner," Mr. Roberts spoke up. "We need to welcome this young lady to our fold." He looked at Deidre. "In fact, I've heard Wyndham speak of a new poetess who was going to join us."

This got Wyndham's attention back on track to Deidre. "Yes, Deidre dear, what is that delicious poem going to be about that you have prepared for us?"

Deidre tried not to blush. "The mechanics of love."

"Love? What kind of subject is that for the new century?" Edward interrupted.

"Love is important to all things," Henri countered. "Love is an ingredient essential to all art."

Deidre defended her subject. "Love is like oxygen. It breathes life into any art."

"Here, here." Roberts raised his glass to her. "I think you found a good catch in this one, Wyndham."

"Of course, Roberts. When have I ever been wrong about inviting anyone into our select group?"

A gong sounded and a footman stood in the doorway. "Dinner is served." The call for dinner rang through the salon as the small groups started to move toward that end.

Henri moved toward Deidre and offered his arm to her. "May I escort you into dinner, my dear?"

Deidre smiled at his warm offering. "I'd be delighted, Mr. Gaudier."

"You can call me Henri."

She tried not to blush as he said it. This was the second Henri that she was to be researching. She was hoping she'd do a better job of her observations than with Henri Toulouse-Lautrec in

Paris. Though as she looked him over, she couldn't help wondering what he'd be like with his hands. She so loved sculptors.

She caught Max's eye as Henri escorted her into dinner. She wasn't sure, but it looked like he had fire in his eyes. He couldn't be jealous. This was her assignment, and he knew that. She couldn't shake the feeling, as Henri pulled her chair out for her, that Max was watching her every move.

The dinner courses were interspersed with the delightful chatter of her fellow artists. She sat between two men, one being Henri, the other being Ezra. Max was seated across from her, flanked by two women, Helen and a new member she didn't recognize. She was glad to know the women in the group were growing in number.

In fact, she turned to Henri to talk about them. She thought it was a good subject to start a conversation with him. "Why is it that women are so left out of the arts?"

Henri finished his bite and wiped his mouth with his napkin. "I'm not sure, except that maybe women are not considered the proper visionaries in most professions. A woman's place is usually in the home. When would there be time for art?"

Her head was already starting to hurt from the silly stereotype. What could she do to unhinge the men? "What if women stopped being in the home and moved into the work place? It would give them satisfaction as well."

Ezra heard her comment and added, "And I suppose you would insist that women vote next?" He seemed startled by her suggestion.

She continued. "Of course. Women are limited by society because men run it. We're told to not do something and brainwashed that we'd be better off staying in the home. Really. I think it's time to clean up the ways of men, and come up with more original ideas on how to run the world."

Henri gave a small laugh. "And how would you run the world, Deidre?"

Max lifted his chin from the conversation he was having with Helen Sanders. In fact, it seemed a lot of the table conversation was quieting to hear her answer. "It's simple, Henri. Men would have to do what women told them to, instead of the other way around. Men could take care of the children just as easily as the women. In fact, it would be easier. Shifts could be established. Women could take their place in factories and switch back and forth between the home and work. The elder women unfit for labor could care for the children."

She felt she was on a roll. Everyone's gaze was upon her now. She thought she'd go full tilt with her ideas. No harm in planting the seed of what was to happen in the future anyway. "With a larger work force and the elderly being useful, there would be time for more fun and games. School could be longer for all children to learn. They wouldn't need to work for their families."

Henri began to clap. "Bravo, Deidre. I think the world according to your vision would be a good start to get the mechanics of the new age on its way."

"But what about war, famine, disease?" Ezra ticked off each item on his hand as if it were a grocery list.

"War would be less common. Men would be kept busy doing something else."

The women laughed at this, and a couple of the men around the table joined in. Henri prodded. "Go on, what else?"

Deidre took a deep breath, giving strength to her words. "Famine would be averted if we had all hands trying to feed the masses. With new machines to farm, it will be easier to produce more crops. I have faith in this inventive age. Machines will just be the start of the progress."

She looked around the room to see everyone's rapt attention. "Disease would be averted as the inventive minds of the age developed more medicines that would cure polio and consumption." She dared not call tuberculosis by name. She was relieved she could remember this period's term for it.

Henri raised his glass. "The horrors of the world solved by the enchanting mind of our beautiful Deidre."

"Yes, my dear." Ezra grabbed her hand. "I do so love the infectious pull of your mind toward the positive."

"It's what my father says is her greatest virtue." Max's eyes were alight with admiration across from her.

Wyndham interrupted the revelry. "On that note, it is time to hear more of our ideas and visions for this new age. Come. Let us reconvene in the parlor to hear what some of our artists have prepared for us."

Deidre had a feeling of dread deep within the pit of her stomach. "So soon? I thought I'd have some time to prepare."

"Oh no, dear. It's a friendly sharing of our ideas. Sort of a summary of what to expect." Helen's voice sounded like she was a teacher correcting Deidre's wrong answer.

"Oh, right. I see."

Henri added, "Eventually a round of games, too. Tonight is for relaxing and getting to know each other some more." He pulled out her chair, and she stood. "I'd be happy to show you the lay of the land."

She placed her hand in Henri's. "Thank you. I'm feeling a bit bewildered by all of this. I've never been considered an artist before." She saw the others getting up from the table and making their way to an adjacent parlor. They moved through the dining room doorway.

This room had a much lighter and airier feel. A blazing fire lit the room, and gas sconces mounted on the oak-paneled walls offered added warmth. Plush cushioned chairs and couches formed a semicircle in front of the fireplace. Henri guided Deidre to the crème-colored couch facing back to the dining room, and then sat next to her. Max had escorted the new woman, with Helen being led over by Wyndham. The other men gathered standing near the settee or near the mantel. The women sat on chairs and the settee. A butler proceeded around to the men with sifters of brandy and port.

"Do I not get to try some?" Deidre asked.

Henri had a gleam in his eye as he smiled at Deidre. "Do you like port?"

"Yes. I love it. I've never sipped a good English port. Mostly Spanish and French." The butler, hearing her interest, arrived with his tray. She took one of the small crystal snifters. Henri joined her, clinking to her health.

She liked being closer to him on the couch. She sat next to him. She sipped her port, looking him over. His suit gave him a slim shape. His gentle hands had calluses from his work with sculpture. But the fine material and tailoring of his suit told her he was of means at the very least. He was charming. It was a shame that he would die in the war. Maybe she could do something about that. She tried to shake off that thought. The port must be affecting her thinking already.

Her thoughts were interrupted when Wyndham tapped his crystal snifter with an ornate ring on his finger. All eyes turned to him standing near the mantel. "If I may have your attention. It is time to do introductions of what we have prepared for this weekend's meeting." He put his arm to his side while holding his port glass, and spoke. "As the leader of the Vorticists, I welcome you all to John Spencer's family estate." There was a polite applause. "He will be joining us tomorrow since his business has made him extend his stay in London. But he wishes everyone to get comfortable and ready for this gathering."

"To our host. He breathes life into our work," Ezra added, raising his glass.

"Like love," Henri whispered while eyeing Deidre. She couldn't help but smile. She tried not to think of how it would feel to kiss him. Well, at least not yet.

"First, I give the floor to Ezra. What do you have for us this weekend, my friend?"

Ezra cleared his throat and sat up. "I've been considering the mechanics of friendship and relationships. A lot can be said for someone who supports you. Just as a bridge needs the correct arch or support, so do all of us. Foundation is the ingredient to all that humans find holy."

There was a gentle applause as Wyndham waved a hand toward William Roberts. "And William. What portraits did you bring to share?"

"I have brought some examples of a new style that derives from lines of geometric shape corresponded in the face. Showing all the planes and angles hinting at the real form, giving an inkling of what you would actually see."

Deidre started to drift as Wyndham called on different members. She noticed Max staring at her, his face a mask, hiding what he was thinking. It made her feel awkward, almost like she had done something wrong. Whatever was the matter with him? He seemed to be getting to know the mystery woman well enough. Being close with the Vorticists was going to make their mission much simpler.

Polite applause interrupted her thoughts as Wyndham called on the next person. "Deidre."

She noticed all eyes on her suddenly. She cleared her throat. "Oh well, yes. I have planned to share a piece about the mechanics of love."

"A most difficult subject, Deidre." Helen's berating voice poked at her intellect. "How do you ever expect to cover such a subject?"

"Deidre just needs to present the workings of love, not the answer," Henri stepped in to answer. "That should be left to each and every one individually."

Helen smiled. "Oh, I see. Each should choose whom to love and how. Especially if they could never love you."

Henri eyed her. "Especially that. No one can choose whom they love."

"I beg to differ. It is a choice to love," Ezra piped into the debate.

"Love is not a choice. It's a right," Wyndham added. "A right to be earned."

"No. Love has no meaning unless you have found it with someone first." Max got all eyes to turn to him with his statement.

"You speak as if from experience," Henri commented.

Deidre watched Max look at her as he spoke next. "It is a curse that is enjoyed only after you first have found that someone to love. And it is a blessing if they love you back."

"And I gather you've had both?" Henri was leaning on Deidre, pressing his leg into hers.

Max didn't look at Henri, but still at Deidre. "Yes. I've known the double-edged sword called love."

"This will prove to be an interesting meeting for us all." Wyndham gained control of the conversation again. Proceeding with more introductions, he moved onto another painter. The mysterious woman was revealed to be Jessica Dismorr. Deidre was distracted from the introductions by Henri's hand easing onto her thigh.

She turned to see his eyes looking deep into her own. His soul was speaking through them. She did long to kiss him, run her fingers along his collarbone, and feel him within her. It had been over a month since her last encounter to charge her bracelet.

She put her hand over Henri's caressing fingers. As she took a sip of port, she noticed Max staring at her. She chose to ignore him. She had her mission. Henri rubbed her hand back with his fingertips. He was touching her. It was a start.

"That concludes our meeting for tonight." Wyndham was wrapping up the talk. Deidre turned away from Henri to see what he had to finish with. "We'll be meeting after breakfast tomorrow to hear some of the work from our poets. Deidre and Ezra will be sharing their stirring projects." There was a polite applause as people looked her way. She began to feel queasy and lightheaded. She wasn't sure if it was the port or the fact she'd have to read her poem tomorrow.

"Are you all right, Deidre?" The edge of concern in Henri's voice was touching.

"I'm afraid I'm feeling a bit lightheaded."

"Maybe some fresh air would help. We can go for a walk in the garden if you like?"

"Yes, that would be good. Thank you."

He helped her up and guided her through a hallway off the parlor to an adjoining room that had double doors. It seemed to be a garden room, with walls and ceilings made of glass panes. "We'll cut through the conservatory to the back gardens. It should help clear your head." He held the door open as she walked through.

The scent of fresh gardenias was in the air, and Deidre breathed it in. "Thank you. The air is helping. I am feeling better already."

"While we're out here, we can go for a stroll." His voice was gentle.

"That would be nice." She accepted Henri's offered arm, and they headed down the path from the conservatory. Low shrubs marked the edges, with gravel strewn along the path. A bright half moon lit the sky. Crickets sang, lending their mysterious peaceful sounds to the moment. Deidre felt tingles through her body where Henri was clasping her arm. She wanted to keep this going as long as she could.

They strolled for a while, not saying a word. The darkness of the night enveloped them, almost cradling them in comfort. They came to a clearing among the trees where a wrought-iron bench welcomed them beneath a trellis of climbing pink roses in bloom. Deidre headed toward it, guiding Henri to sit next to her. She couldn't help but stare into his brown eyes. They wove her into a spell, and she got lost in them. He was her mission, after all. The Time Council's rules played in her head, "Get close but not too close."

Henri broke the spell by saying, "It is a lovely evening for a stroll."

"Yes it is." She didn't notice that they were clasping hands still. It just seemed natural to do so. "I didn't know England could be so lovely."

"It can be. It's as if the elves and fairies have woven a perfect night just for us."

Deidre felt the breath catch in her chest. Her thoughts froze in anticipation. Henri edged closer. She leaned forward, knowing that the brush of his lips would be the ultimate dessert to cap off the evening. She stopped just before his mouth. Looking at him she said, "I didn't know that an evening could be so sublime."

"You are sublime, my beautiful Deidre." She felt his hand reach behind her head and pull her toward him. She let him kiss her lips with the hint of pressure, relishing the connection of intimacy. So very typical of this age. Everything was so gentle, so subtle.

She knew she had to keep her pouncing urges to a minimum. But she couldn't resist his lush lips. She pressed gently against them, feeling him equal her pressure. It was the green light to reach toward him and caress his face, achieving a connection with her newest subject.

They moved closer, encouraged by the kiss, meshing their bodies as close as possible. Had Deidre a bed, she might have thrown him upon it. But she was supposed to be demure. She needed to play that part to the hilt. She moved back and had the decency to blush. A kiss in this age was equivalent to full copulation in her age. But in its own way, this subtle declaration of intimacy was making her heart race as much as him being inside her. It made her want him all the more because of it.

Henri held her, speaking in a whisper. "Deidre, I cannot keep myself from you. You are something akin to an elixir of love. I could become addicted to your company."

She felt warmth in her face. Was it his humble declaration inducing her to fall for him? She wasn't sure. This age could be so confusing in its subtle foreplay. "You compel me to ask for one more kiss."

Henri took her in an embrace. His lips met hers. She gave herself over to the passion of their kiss. She longed to have his hands caress her entire body, like her Parisian sculptor. But could the English be that passionate? She heard a rustle in the bushes near her, and Henri pulled away.

She turned to see Max with Jessica Dismorr on his arm. She had been caught in an embrace with a man. This was very embarrassing for the time, especially since Max was supposed to be her brother. But she didn't pull away. She had to play this as the stubborn sister for the others involved. If she could have communicated privately with Max, she would have told him that she was getting somewhere with her mission target and shooed him away.

Max cleared his throat. "Pardon our intrusion." His stern voice led to a gasp from Jessica Dismorr. Drawing her arms away from Henri would be the right thing. But Deidre didn't want to lose the contact. Henri took the cue from her and didn't pull away, either. They held their pose, a testimony to their budding emotions for the intruders to witness.

Jessica's mouth drew into a smile when they didn't move. "We'll be leaving now." Jessica Dismorr had the decency to gauge the situation and turn to leave them alone. But Max didn't try to turn. He stared at them, the hurt dawning in his eyes. Deidre knew she had to say something to keep their cover.

"It is a beautiful night for a stroll, brother dear." She tried to stress the word brother to Max. He had to remember the role he played in their research charade.

There was a pause as he seemed to mull over the situation. He pursed his lips and bent down near Jessica's ear. "We should leave them alone. Come along."

Jessica didn't hesitate, but followed Max's lead. Deidre saw him turn once and saw the longing in his eyes. She knew in that instant that it was hard for him to watch her with Henri. Because, after all, he wasn't really her brother. Maybe all that talk of love had been real. But for whom? Was he pretending to pursue Jessica for the same research motives as she was pursuing Henri? Was she jealous? Did she want to be with Max and take Jessica's place? She shook off the idea. After watching them go, she turned to Henri. "Where were we?"

"You were my elixir?"

She kissed him, drawing his lower lip into her mouth. If only she could take him, but she needed to draw him into her seduction slowly. It was all in the name of research. But her mind kept drifting to her new partner, Max. As her lips lay on another man's mouth, she thought of what it would be like to kiss Max again instead. Was he making her lose her focus? She batted thoughts of Max from her mind and concentrated on Henri. But as she felt Henri's hands caress her back, she found herself imagining they belonged to Max.

Twelve

Breakfast was a buffet of cheeses, breads, meats, cutlets, and coffee. Deidre managed to get enough food, and she even managed to get it to stay down. Which wasn't easy. Her stomach kept doing flips. She was so nervous.

They were still finishing up the meal. Henri sat to one side of her with Max on the other. She wasn't sure if she could leave the table. If only she would stop thinking about what everyone might think about her poem. She couldn't get the image of them laughing at her out of her head. It was paralyzing her.

"Are you all right, Deidre? You are looking a bit green." Max placed his hand on her wrist.

His tone gently brushed her nerves away. "Yes, I'm fine. Just a bit nervous."

"They'll love your poem. Who could resist you?" Henri said to next to her. "Especially when you recite about a subject so controversial."

"But will they like it?" she asked.

Henri said, "They'll love it. Coming from you, I'm sure."

She managed to blush. "Max has heard the start of it. He didn't say it was horrible."

"Then trust his opinion, Deidre. Try not to worry." Henri patted her hand as though she were a child. She wanted to wrench it away. But she figured he was treating her as women in this time were treated. Sometimes that alone churned her stomach.

"Of course, I could recite the one about Paris. I do so miss it." Her head was swimming with indecision.

"Whichever you choose to share, it will be wonderful," Max whispered quickly. He rose from the table.

Deidre froze. She had always been the observer of art. Not one of the artists. She didn't know if she could get up. Max stood next to her, wiped the corners of his mouth, and left the napkin on the table. He took a moment watching her. "Are you going to stand?"

"Do I have to?"

Max put his hand on her shoulder. "They are both good, Deidre. You will not disappoint them."

"But will they like it?" Her voice wavered.

"They're English. They'll have to pretend they do. So don't worry." He bent closer to her ear so only she could hear. "You wanted to be the artist, remember? It's part of the role."

She sighed. He was right. She had a job to do. She stood, and Max pulled the chair out for her. They all left the dining room and moved to the conservatory, where the sunshine peeked through the clouds to light the interior. The glass roof and walls gave the whole outdoor effect while keeping bad weather at bay if needed. Today, many of the paneled windows were ajar, letting in fresh air. It gave a romantic anticipation for the poetry to come.

She sat in one of the white wicker chairs. Sinking into the cushion, she remembered to keep her back straight and upright, though her corset helped with the awkward posture. No one could really be fully relaxed in high society, especially in this age. Sitting up was mandatory.

Max stood next to her, tea still in hand. Deidre looked around, noticing the same people as the previous night arrayed around the room. Henri had taken up a chair across from her.

She didn't notice that Max had taken a station next to her until she felt him sit on the corner of the chair. She hoped he didn't play the possessive brother. She had made good progress with Henri last night.

Wyndham clapped twice, gaining everyone's attention. "Today, we will start our meeting with recitations from our poetic members. Deidre Thompson and Ezra Pound will be sharing their poems. Who would like to go first?"

She was relieved to hear Ezra's boisterous voice say he would. He walked to the center of the room, turning to gain everyone's attention. He started out with free verse, bringing a theme of friendship through emotion, a list of instructions based on Aristotle, and contemplation of how it worked in the machine age.

The poem described the use one's friends for profit in industry. It ended on a humorous note comparing the failings of a man to gain a woman's friendship, and giving up. "For men can never truly know how a woman's heart works. Business is business, but a woman is the hardest thing in the world to understand."

There was huge applause as Ezra waved his hand about in thankful bows. Wyndham turned to her. "Deidre, I am looking forward to your work today. Is it on what we talked about last night?"

"Yes. In fact, I might be able to answer Ezra's questioning men's ability to understand women with it. It is on a subject no one understands—love." She stood, taking the paper with her poem carefully scripted on it out of her little purse. She unfolded it carefully and looked up at the people around her. That's when it hit her. Glancing at all the expectant faces, she was overcome with their eyes on her. She felt the swoon hitting her full on, and before she knew it, she found herself on the floor with Max tapping her face lightly, saying her name.

"Water, could someone get her some water?" Henri's anxious voice was in the background.

She tried to move and found that Max had her in his arms. "What happened?"

"You fainted, sister dear. Your nerves seemed to be too much for you."

"It could be the corset." Helen was near, standing over her. Her pursed lips made her voice sound like an old school teacher. "Maybe she should go lie down."

"Good idea." Max helped her to stand. "I can help you get back to your room to lie down. The poem is going to have to wait until another time."

"I'll come help you." She heard Helen's voice behind her.

She let him guide her to the room she stayed in the night before, with Helen guiding her to the bed. Max bid his adieu and let Helen tend to her corset. The relief when Helen released her was welcome. Maybe she had laced it too tightly in her anxiousness this morning. She had wanted everything to be perfect. "There, lie down." Helen brushed her hair back from her eyes once she had her settled in bed. "I'm sure it's a lovely poem. We can always hear it another time."

"Yes. Maybe if I just read from my chair and don't look at everyone." Deidre still felt a bit woozy. Lying back on the pillows more, she said, "I've never done a public reading before."

"It can be a lot for someone their first time. Just rest now. I'll come in later to check on you." Helen closed the drapes and the darkened room seemed soothing. Deidre heard the door open slowly and close. The comfort of the room eased her into sleep. She felt safe. She didn't realize she was asleep until she awoke later to hear someone going about her room. "Who's there?"

Max came over to the bed. "It's me, sister dear. I persuaded Helen that I needed to check on you, because I'm family and all." He sat next to her on the bed. "You gave everyone quite a scare. Fainting like that. Hell, you gave me a scare. You feeling all right?"

His hand clasped hers lying on top of the comforter.

"Yes. I feel fine now. It could have been the corset." She squeezed back. "I didn't know what to expect. Fainting wasn't on my radar of things to go wrong. I'm sorry, Max."

He patted her hand. "Not to worry. You gave it a go. Maybe you're right that you should read it sitting down, and under less formal surroundings. What about the parlor we were in last night?"

"Yes. Maybe somewhere familiar." She pulled her hand away from Max and pushed herself up a little. "Maybe I'll need a glass of port to loosen me up a bit."

"Yes. Well. It would, I'm sure." Max's face looked distant for a moment.

"Is there something wrong?" It was Deidre's turn to hold his hand. It was subtle but brought him back to her.

He looked down at her hand. "Henri. I'm concerned about you getting too close to him." He didn't raise his head.

She knew this was a bad sign. "But I need to study him. It's the best way sometimes—to get involved with the artist."

"But not too involved." He looked her in the eye. "That's what I'm worried about. Observation, casual flirtations and interactions if need be. But never anything serious."

"I'm aware of the timeanaut code. Intimacy is only required if I need to charge my bracelet crystal. I always try to not choose the main study subject for that. But mostly, utilize my partner." She looked away from him when she realized what she'd said.

"Exactly." Something more was in his voice. Urgent need radiated from him. "And I'm not sure if you're aware of how dangerous it can be if you do not. Things that can be changed."

She looked back at him. There was hurt reflected in his eyes. "I am well aware. I've seen it happen, and the price James paid."

Max grimaced. "I'm sorry. I didn't want to bring up James. I'm going to miss him too."

"You knew him?" He took a moment to look away. Something was definitely bothering him. Deidre knew she owed him at least a moment to confide. "What is it really Max? You can tell me what's bothering you. I'm your partner now, after all."

He looked back at her, then again looked away. She could see the tension in his face as his jaw muscles flexed. "I lied, Deidre. About the Council. They didn't approve my travel here. In fact, they were ready to forfeit your life for their precious timeline."

She leaned toward him, grabbing his hand. "What do you mean?"

He finally looked her in the eyes. "I mean, that I didn't have permission to come. Or even to save you. I came…" He paused, looking away again.

She squeezed his hand. "Go on."

"I came to save you." He turned to her, his face intense and full of emotion. "Because I'm in love with you."

She blinked, holding his hand tighter. There was a charge between them. Something electric brought him emotionally closer. It seemed like the air crackled between them. She answered, "Max. I didn't know."

"After James was lost, I knew I couldn't hold my feelings back." He caressed her hand. "And you headed into your next jump before I could send a message through Ops. Then, it came up in the timeline what you had done. You changed history with your actions here. The Council needed to fix it. That fix killed you." He shook his head, looking down at her hand. He caressed it again. "I couldn't let it happen."

Her eyes grew wide. "You mean you defied Time Council Law and came to change their correction?"

"Yes. I had to save you. Those brutes would have killed you. Their plan fixed the timeline to ensure you never met Henri. Because you see…" He looked down for a moment and back to her eyes. "You fell in love with him and stopped him from going to war. He lives instead of dying. It makes his art become more obscure, and the impact on history could not be fixed by any other means." He looked back into her eyes. "The Council ruled you had to die for your actions. They deemed you a Time Rogue."

This time, she pulled her hand away from him, gasping. "Max, what have you done?"

"Yes. I know." He leaned into her, pressing his forehead against hers. "I couldn't lose you. It would have been the death of me."

Her breath brushed his lips. "What are we going to do?"

His lips were tantalizingly close. He pulled away and spoke firmly. "First, we need to finish the poetry reading. Follow the mission without you getting involved with Henri. It might appease the Council to have the timeline fixed this way."

"And if it doesn't work?" Deidre's voice didn't hold back her fear.

He reached for both her hands and looked her in the eyes. "We will be Time Rogues, and we'll have to avoid the Council's agents." His voice started coming out in a rush. "It was the only way to save you, Deidre. I couldn't lose you again. I love you too much."

The pull was too great for them. His lips touched hers, feather light, seeking her response. She closed her eyes and reached for him. Pulling him close, she wanted more. No one had sacrificed something like this for her. Without him, she knew she'd be dead. Their lips played in the dance of discovered emotions, pulling on each other as the passion grew.

His hands wrapped around her. She could feel her need building, this man embracing her, pressing himself against her. She felt herself sliding into dangerous territory. She was starting to lose herself with him.

Their chests pressed against each other and she was captured by his weight pushing her toward an all but uncontrollable desire. Something she wanted from him more than ever now. She wrapped her arms around his neck, driving her fingers through his hair as they kissed. His hands sought her below her clothes, exploring her body's curves under her blouse.

Her legs moved to wrap around his, hugging their bodies closer. "Max, wait."

"Yes?"

"Lord knows, I want you now."

"I know." He kissed her again, losing them both again in their passion.

She put her hand to his face to stop him. "But it's dangerous here. Brothers and sisters don't do this. It will blow our cover."

He kissed her one more time and leaned back. "I can't keep myself from you."

She pressed her hand to his lips. "I know. But if we're found like this, we'll never finish the mission and fix the timeline."

"Damn it." He eased off of her. "But when we get back to our room at the inn, I can't be blamed for what I'll do to you there."

"I want you too." She pulled him back down to her.

He returned the gesture, putting his fingers to her lips. "I'll leave you to rest." He eased back and got off the bed. "You think you'll be up to reading the poem tonight?"

She took a deep breath to steady herself. "The port sounds like a good idea. Maybe it's just that I'm not a morning person."

He laughed. "No. Artists tend not to be. Have a rest, sister dear." He caressed her hair, lingering around her face. "Rest, my love."

She nodded as he patted her cheek. "Remember how much I love you." He turned, moving to the door. "Maybe you'll have more to draw from for other poems now."

Deidre laughed this time. "I think I'm going to be able to write a book after all this. Maybe my next assignment should be a writer."

"If we get out of this, I'll try to make it so. Rest." He went through the door, closing it gently. Deidre felt her eyes growing heavy just from the revelations of the last few moments.

Max loved her. Her thoughts only paused for a moment. It didn't hurt as much to think of James. She was wondering what the difference was as the sweet scent of the garden came through the window to help her sleep. The one thing that nagged at the back of her mind was the locket. The picture in it would drift into her mind as the fragrances outside lulled her. Where did it come from? Who had sent it? What did it mean?

Those questions kept destroying everything until she remembered Max's lips on hers. Her mind drifted back to Max, kissing her, holding her. It was thoughts of him that relaxed her enough to fall asleep as the afternoon sunshine spilled through the window.

Thirteen

Deidre held the paper. Its fluttering edge gave away her nervousness. She had only just finished a glass of port before standing to face everyone, and still felt flush from it. Max had been right. It did help. Deidre looked to Max, and he smiled. She nodded as a loving sister should, gaining encouragement from her brother. Then, she looked to Henri. She tried to not get lost in his delicious gaze. She wondered if being warned was going to stop her heart from falling for him. She licked her lips before she began.

"Tonight I have a poem on a slippery subject. Love. I don't profess to be an expert on this subject, just an avid student." She cleared her throat and looked about the room. She could see Helen by Wyndham, her hand very close to his. Jessica sat across, eyelids hooded as she looked at her. The other men looked attentive, and Henri encouraged her, "Go on." She looked to Max. He nodded.

Holding up his glass of scotch, Ezra said, "As are we all, my dear. I'm sure no one considers themselves to be an expert. Have at your poem."

She cleared her throat and looked down at the paper. She decided it would be best not to look at the eyes watching her. She could look at the paper, the wooden floor of the parlor, and the tops of her shoes. That could be her focus as she read. Nothing else. She looked down and began.

"Forever Frozen
It began,
A few summers ago.
Late one evening,
He was there.
Making my heart flutter.
Little did my heart know,
The trouble and pain,
As he left me that day,
To never return.
Forever I long,
For his touch, his lips,
His breath near me,
Whispering in my ear,
That fateful day,
'I love you, Deidre, forever.'
Never to return,
To whisper them again.
My heart will never
Beat the same.
It stands still

Like in a frozen pond
Never reaching spring thaw,
Forever frozen,
From the touch of his lips,
On mine.
Never to return,
Never to return."

She looked up to the sound of light applause around the room. Smiles greeted her instead of laughter. She let out the breath she was holding, feeling a weight drift away from her into the floor.

John was at the other end of the mantel, clapping and smiling. He spoke first. "Deidre, I loved your poem. It moved me."

Ezra spoke next. "That was wonderful, my dear." He came over and grabbed her around the arm. "You had nothing to fear. It was gripping. Truly capturing the heart ache of that torturous love."

"Yes, it was quite dramatic." Helen's quiet voice added to the compliments. "I was living the anguish as you read."

Deidre turned to speak a thank you as Henri spoke. "I can only imagine who it was that broke your heart. How brave of you to share it. I can see now why it was difficult."

"Yes. I was wary to share this." She put her hand up to her mouth to hold back the emotion, taking a moment to steady herself. "It is so personal."

Wyndham stepped forward. "But that is why it's so grand. It's real, expressing the loneliness of waiting for someone who may return."

Deidre blinked. "What do you mean 'may return'?"

"Why, my dear, it may be what you're missing. The hope that he may return. Surely, you haven't given up."

"Wyndham, don't be so cruel." Helen's voice held a caring tone.

"I assume it is about a real man, then?" Wyndham still pressed with his questioning.

"Yes."

"Then, he is beyond saving?"

"He was my betrothed." She took a breath. "He died."

"There. No hope for returning then," Ezra chimed in.

"You both are horribly inconsiderate of her feelings." Henri tried to head off their comments. "She just bared her soul for us."

Deidre looked toward him and nodded. "Thank you, Henri. That's so kind of you to say."

Henri's defense did him credit in Deidre's mind. She smiled his way, and saw Max looking at her, hurt in his eyes. "My heart has not been the same, and won't be, until I find another to make me feel as James did."

Ezra clapped. "That's it. That's the ending. Say something like, 'Without another to thaw it, I am lost. I look toward the end of this lonely winter.'"

"That does have a good ring to it." Wyndham tapped the edge of his glass of scotch.

John moved away from the other side of the mantel where he'd been listening. "If you want to take a break, we can."

"No, I have one more poem. I finished a new one right after my nap." She looked at Max. "I was inspired by coming here."

The men sat back down, reclining, while John stayed standing by the mantel. She took another piece of paper from her purse, and took a deep, cleansing breath. This time she looked at everyone, stopping on Max where she began to read.

> *"Summer has returned.*
> *Now that he smiles at me.*
> *Never has sunshine*
> *Felt like this.*
> *Not since he*
> *That was lost*
> *Forever*
> *Departed.*
> *He that shines*
> *To me now,*
> *Gives me new hope,*
> *A radiance.*
> *He has melted*
> *The frozen center*
> *Of my heart.*
> *It beats again."*

She looked up from the paper. "I haven't given it a title yet." Deidre smiled at Henri, and then her eyes drifted back to Max.

Henri sat straighter, while Max held her gaze. Deidre looked first back to Henri, and then to Max. She smiled as a silence hung over the room. She asked, "What did you think?"

Ezra put his glass down on the end table and moved to her, clasping her arms. "You are a true poetess, my dear." He kissed each of her cheeks. "You have put me in my place tonight. If you put those together, you may have it."

Deidre turned to see Helen with a tear in her eye, wiping it with a small kerchief. "So this means it's good?"

Ezra patted her arms again. "Very good." He turned to everyone in the parlor. "I think we have a new member of our group." He grabbed his glass off of the end table. "To Deidre, the newest Vorticist!"

"To Deidre." Everyone raised their glasses. Deidre felt her smile was going to stay that way forever. Her very insides felt ready to explode with pride. She wasn't observing anymore. She was an artist.

She moved to sit next to Henri, feeling Max's eyes follow her to the position on the couch.

"Should we have a game now?" John moved to where Deidre had stood and faced his guests.

"Yes. That sounds like fun." Deidre clapped her hands, relief flooding through her now that her reading was over.

"Something more sophisticated than our normal drinking games, I hope. We have ladies present." Henri motioned to Deidre next to him.

Wyndham crossed his legs, relaxing back on the cushioned couch. "What about Twenty Questions?"

John moved to the mantel and tapped it. "I don't know Wyndham, last time we played that, you kept betting on how many questions it would take. And if I remember right, you weren't very good at it."

Everyone laughed, creating an awkward ripple of noise that ended with everyone taking a sip of their drink. Ezra snapped his fingers. "I've got it. How about 'Sculptor'? We can have Henri start for us. And have two lumps for him to sculpt at a time."

"Oh, it's been forever since we've tried that," Jessica said in response to Ezra's suggestion, perking up next to Max.

Henri got up, looking over his potential lumps. He put his hand to his chin, supporting his elbow with his other arm, in a quiet, pensive pose. He pointed to Helen and John. Helen stood up, standing over near the fireplace at the center of the room with John. Henri moved to John, positioning his arm up high, and his hand in a scratching position under his arm.

Deidre chuckled and then put a hand over her mouth. "Oh, I'm sorry I didn't mean to laugh." She put her hand down.

Wyndham exclaimed, "That's it, Deidre. If you start laughing first, it might get the lumps to join in."

Ezra encouraged her. "We play hard ball games here. Any disadvantage you can offer is welcome."

Max tried to rescue her. "I think my sister may not be familiar with this game or maybe the way it's played here."

Ezra answered, "If either lump laughs, Deidre, that one will be the sculptor next, and choose a new lump of clay to take their place."

"See, sister dear, they do play it similar to us in the States." Max motioned in agreement with Ezra.

Deidre nodded, realizing Max had saved her. She had forgotten that people in the past entertained themselves in such arcane ways. Silly, it seemed. But she could see why they had to. With no virtual display, they had to create all the entertainment themselves. This may prove to be more interesting research than having to write her poem.

She took a sip of port, watching the concentration in Henri's face. If only he weren't so good-looking. His face looked so gorgeous, with the lock of hair falling a little into his eyes as he moved Helen's hand into an Egyptian dancer's gesture. He lifted one arm and turned her hand to point out, and positioned her bottom arm to point at an opposite angle. To her credit, Helen remained stone-faced.

Ezra started to sing. "I'm a little teapot, short and stout." Henri turned to look at him and smiled. He snapped his fingers. He turned back to John and positioned his arms to resemble a teapot, then pushed his back down for him to lean. Everyone then joined in except for the two statues. "Here is my handle, here is my spout."

John was holding the position, not faltering, but Henri turned to Helen. He bent her over and moved her spout to pour over John. Laughter roared through the room as the singing continued. "When I get steamed up, hear me shout. Tip me over, and pour me out."

With the last line, Helen held her hand right over John's backside and turned bright red. Her smile broke her face, and she giggled, losing the game. She moved her hands over her face, and broke into a full laugh.

John stood up and went to stretch. Ezra pointed at him. "No fair. You're still a statue, John. Helen needs to pick her new lump of clay."

John returned to his position, an over exaggerated expression on his face showed how much he was enjoying it. Helen looked about the room and pointed at Max. "You. You shall be my lump."

Max rose, placed his glass down on the end table, and walked up next to John. "Mold me, dear sculptor."

"I intend to. I will turn you into a beautiful masterpiece." Helen flipped her hand in the air in a fanfare gesture. Laughter surrounded her as she grabbed Max's arm and held it above John's buttocks. She bent down and turned John's head to see Max in swing formation, and he fell over laughing.

"Oh, John, you're no fun. I wasn't done yet." Helen's reprimand was laughed at even more.

"Oh, but I was, dear woman. I was." John laughed as he brushed himself off and scouted the group for his lump of clay. Helen returned to her seat next to Wyndham when John's eyes set on Deidre. "Come here, my dear. I believe you are the perfect lump to sculpt."

Deidre stood and walked to stand next to Max. He still was in the bent over position, one hand poised to swat. She stood across from him, and John took her arm. She froze, letting him guide her hand to be a mirror of Max's. Then, he leaned her toward Max. He moved to the other side of Max, and moved him closer as well, pushing him toward her face and lips. Little by little, John angled them closer so they were staring into each other's eyes, their hands up to block what would be a possible kiss.

Deidre wanted to win. She was determined not to laugh. But staring at Max, and how he looked at her, it wasn't funny at all. He was enjoying looking at her, getting closer, she knew by his face. In fact, as both their hands were moved toward the other, she was wishing they could kiss.

But it would lose the game. And she was sure neither of them wanted to lose. But when John moved their faces so they were cheek to cheek, the room was in an uproar. She was brought back into the moment, realizing people were watching. A blush filled her face, and she laughed. Damn. She hated losing.

It left Max in a precarious position. He had to hold form, leaning down, his head to the side where hers had been. She looked around the room to decide who would be the funniest cheek to cheek with Max. "You. Ezra, are the perfect lump of clay for me."

"Oh, I think we've had enough fun with this game." Ezra patted away the suggestion with his hand.

"No," Wyndham said. "You suggested we play this. You will get up and play, man. Get to it."

Ezra placed his glass down. "Fine. I will be the most perfect lump wished for by any sculptor."

He walked up next to Max, and Deidre looked him over. With hands on her hips, she walked around Ezra to view him from different angles.

"Get on with it. I'm a very impatient lump." Chuckles circled the room from Ezra's comment.

Deidre moved to get Max to stand. She didn't want him to hurt himself. She reached under his arms to manipulate how he stood, swinging him into a twist. She felt the undeniable attraction, her body rubbing next to him. Her breasts pressed against his back. She would have stayed like that if she could. She could breathe in his masculine scent. She could not blush this close to her brother. She dared not linger this way.

She moved to Ezra and put up his hands, curling his fingers to make it look like he was inviting a fight. She smiled as she moved back to Max, putting his hands up in mock surrender. She even started touching his face to try to manipulate it into a surprise look. He broke up laughing when she was trying to move his mouth into an "O" of shock.

"You got me, sister dear." He patted her on the back as she went to sit down. He looked around the room for his lump. His eyes rested on Henri. "I don't believe you've had a turn to be a lump yet."

Max curled his finger calling Henri forward. Henri brushed himself off and straightened his jacket. "Do be kind."

"Don't worry, ole boy. I'll sculpt out your true form."

Everyone chuckled as Max pointed where he wanted Henri to stand. Ezra had kept his fisticuff fighting pose the whole time. He was playing to win. Max put up Henri's fists in a similar pose. He changed Ezra's position to lean back and take a punch, freezing them both in a tableau of a gentlemen's quarrel. When neither broke up from the pose, Max tried moving Ezra to strike Henri back. He had them posed in a moment before Ezra's fist connected with Henri's jaw. Then, he stood back admiring his work. His hand was on his chin in thought.

"This is horrible. Friends fighting," Deidre exclaimed. "I want a happy ending."

Max snapped his fingers. "Thank you, sister. You gave me an idea."

He moved back to the posed men, pulling their arms back, both raising their hands in salute. Then, he moved their arms, bending them both forward to engage in a hug. Both men began laughing together.

"It's a tie," declared Wyndham. "Well done, Max."

"What does that mean?" Deidre asked.

"It means that is the end. We have a draw. In fact, I am getting a bit tired myself." John stretched as he stood. "If you don't mind, I think I'll retire for the evening."

A trumpet of "Good night, John" farewells followed, with others also taking the cue to retire. Helen followed Wyndham leaving the parlor. Max and Ezra poured themselves another drink, standing by the mantel and starting a conversation.

Henri looked over to Deidre. "Do you want to take a walk, my dear? It's a lovely evening."

Deidre looked away. She tried to not let Henri's eyes enrapture her. She had to be careful now that she knew what could happen. "I don't know."

"It would just be for a moment. Night air is healthy for you. After this morning's episode, I've been so worried about you." He stood and offered his arm. "If I may escort you, I'd be very delighted. You could fill me in on why you wrote that poem. I'm now very curious about this James fellow, and how he could deserve such a wonderful woman."

Deidre thought she heard the hint of jealousy in his voice. "He doesn't compare to you, Henri dear."

"Do be careful, sister dear." Max's voice sounded with concern. "You know you don't want to cause too much stress on your lungs. You remember what happened the last time."

She understood Max's warning. She had to be careful, but she did have a mission to finish. If she could get what the Council wanted without falling for Henri, it could save them both. She offered her hand, and Henri bent to kiss it.

She heard someone clear his throat, and looked over to see Max scowling. She looked back to Henri, his face glowing with passion for her. She was drawn into his eyes. She shouldn't have looked at him. "Yes. I'll go with you for a little while."

She stood, moving out of the room with Henri, not daring to look back at Max. She knew she wouldn't have the nerve if she looked back at him. Henri put out his arm so she could take it. Looping her hand through, he supported her as they walked.

She felt as if she was drifting off the edge of a cliff. Something was attracting her to Henri, almost uncontrollably. She had to fight it for all of them. But she couldn't bear the thought of him dying in the war. All his beauty, his gift of sculpture, would die with him.

He led her to a small opening in the garden, with a small fountain and stone bench. It was a perfect little nook in which to sit. He guided her to the bench. The trickle of the fountain created a mask of peace. But in her heart, Deidre felt a rumbling. She couldn't mask the attraction to Henri. What she knew she had to do was going to be hard. She couldn't fall for him. She had to resist.

Then he looked at her. Henri stared at her, capturing her in his gaze. He held her hands. "I have to confess to you, my dear Deidre. I am captivated by you."

"Really?"

He placed the other hand on hers. "You've taken my heart, my dear. I have fallen deeply and madly for you. You have unfrozen my heart." He leaned toward her. She knew she should turn away. But she wanted him to kiss her. She closed her eyes and felt the sweet caress of his lips. Such a butterfly kiss. Nothing like what she was used to.

"I've waited for this quiet moment in which to tell you something. You are right about needing another to unfreeze one's heart. There was another woman who froze mine as your James froze yours. Now, you have freed me. I hope I can bring that same warmth to yours." He looked into her eyes for an answer.

"I don't know what to say, Henri." She hesitated knowing she had to choose her words carefully. The whole mission's success could rest on this moment. "I am becoming fond of you too."

He kissed her, holding her close. Her whole body responded to him, called by some unseen voice within her. He pulled away and continued. "John supports me in my endeavors, and supplies me with what I need for my craft. Will you join me in it? Join us out here." He wrapped his arms around her, pulling her closer, whispering in her ear. "Stay with us. You can flourish here with your poetry. And your brother is welcome to stay too." His grip around her grew stronger. "Join us."

She closed her eyes as Henri kissed her again. When they pulled apart, she opened her eyes to see Max standing at the entrance of the garden niche. The moonlight illuminated his face in shadow, and he ducked back to hide better when she spotted him.

How dare he follow her. She knew what she was doing. She may have to lead Henri on, but staying at the heart of the Vorticist circle would be invaluable. Max stepped forward shaking his head. So he had heard Henri's offer. She didn't want him to spoil the opportunity. She leaned back. "Yes, Henri. I think that is a brilliant idea."

"Oh, I'm so glad." He hugged her tight.

Max came toward them. "Do you think that is really such a good idea, sister dear?"

Henri moved away quickly, standing to face Max. He coughed awkwardly as Deidre pulled her hands into her lap, curling her fingers. She wasn't sure if he meant the idea of staying or what she had just been doing with Henri. "Max, it would be so much easier to be in the country. Besides, it's such an opportunity for my studies as an artist."

Max was quick to retort. "What do you think Father will say?"

"I know what he'd say, brother dear." She stood and put her hands on her hips. "Do take care to learn as much as you can, Deidre. Seeing the sights of Europe, meeting the people, living as they do. That is pure education."

"I see. You know Father that well." His voice held a hint of misgiving.

"And you'll be with me, dear Max." She walked to him, grabbing his hands. "I don't think I could be any safer than with my family around me."

He whispered closer. "Do you know what you're doing?"

"Do any of us, brother dear?" she whispered back.

"Then it's settled." Henri moved to her and wrapped his arm around her waist. "You'll both be coming to stay here for the time being. I'm sure we can have your things sent from where you're staying."

Max waved his hand. "No, that won't be necessary. I can return and pick up our things, and bring our car out here. I know we didn't plan on being here this long. I assume there is a stable to store our Napier?"

Henri answered, "Of course. John has many resources at his disposal."

"Come then." Max took Deidre's other arm. "You know you can't stay in the night air long. Let's get you back inside." He took her to walk with him, leaving Henri behind. He whispered as he pulled her along. "I need to talk to you when we get inside."

"Of course, brother dear."

He shook his head. "We have a lot to talk about. There are some things I haven't told you yet."

"Like what?" She pulled against his arm. "I'm going along now. You don't have to pull me."

"That was too dangerous. You can't get close to him." He kept up the brisk walk next to her.

She stopped, swinging around to look at him. "Why not? We still need to get the information and finish the mission to fix the timeline."

"Yes. But I must tell you something… Something I wasn't ready to share before."

She put her hands on her hips. "What is it? It couldn't be any worse than dragging me back to the house like this."

"Fine. If it gets you to see reason. You dying in the altered timeline wasn't the only thing that changed. Something else happened."

"Like what?" She crossed her arms.

Max reached out and grasped her around the shoulders and looked her in the eyes. "James is alive."

Fourteen

She felt the shock hit her in the stomach. "What? What do you mean he's alive?"

"When I was on Com that night, I saw you die on the timeline. Then, another agent checked in with Central—one who had previously been dead. It was James." He licked his lips. "You had turned up on the timeline dead, and we lost your signal. Right after that, his signal appeared. It was James, still in the time period he had been left in. But now alive." He swallowed, hesitating to go on. "He checked in with me, thinking you'd made the jump safely. Which you had, but he didn't know what had happened to you later in the timeline."

Her eyes grew wide. "So, my death made him alive?"

"I'm not sure. That's why time travel is so complicated. When one event happens, there seems to be a shift to balance outcomes along the course of time. But then, something might happen to change even that direction of the time flow. That's why time mapping is so important.

I had been watching your time map and had to stop your death when I saw it end. I can't see it now, but whoever is watching your time map will be aware of the repercussions of saving you."

He took a moment to look her over. "The Council thought James reappeared as a correction in the balance, but we're still not always sure why it happens. They wanted to leave it that way." He brought her close to him. Wrapping his arms around her, he tucked her head under his chin. "But I couldn't let you go. James agreed. We came up with a plan."

She spoke in a steady tone, calming her nerves. "You mean you two came up with this whole idea?"

Looking down at her, he put his finger to her lips. "We need to take this inside." They heard the sound of footsteps behind them. He raised his voice. "I'll take you back to your room, sister dear. I don't want you catching your death of cold."

He wrapped his arm around her waist, guiding her up the steps to the main house, and into the warmth of the main hall. They turned down a side corridor and took the stairs up to their rooms. Deidre made a straight shot to her room, and Max followed her in. He turned to close the door as she sat on the bed.

She folded her arms, arranging a pout on her face. "Now you've got to tell me everything. Come clean, Max. What the hell else happened?"

"You look adorable when you're mad."

"Don't try to distract me. Out with it, Max."

He sat next to her on the bed. "James thought it had something to do with the balance. A life for a death. Matter has to balance in some way. Once you died, he was able to live."

Just hearing James's name again made her stomach flip. She took a deep breath to settle it. "Does it reverse?"

"It may. There is still research going on about this phenomenon. It is why timeanauts have to be so careful." He put his hand to her face, leaving it on her cheek. "But I know James and I would both trade our lives for you."

She grabbed his hand. "Tell me. What else did he say?"

"That he would find a way to contact me once I arrived to this time. He was still in the year of your last assignment, 1884. He was going to try to jump to this date and contact me in some way."

She cocked a brow and gave him a curious look. "You wouldn't think a locket would be a way to communicate."

"What do you mean, a locket?"

"I received a locket from a strange man when I got to the tea shop."

"What? The one you had on earlier?"

Deidre undid the top buttons of her blouse, reached in, and pulled out the silver locket on its chain. "It's got James's picture in it."

"That must be the communication. Could I look at it for a second?"

"Sure." She reached behind her neck and undid the locket. She pulled it off and lowered it into his waiting palm.

Gripping the locket, he said, "I don't know what's in this, but I know one thing. I won't let anyone hurt you." He turned it in his fingers, inspecting all sides.

"I know. Go ahead. Find out what he wants us to know."

He looked down, turning the locket once more. "There's only the initials J.D. on the back."

She tapped the locket. "There's his picture inside, remember."

He levered the locket open, and both could see the tintype of a light-haired man. His serious look was typical of picture portraits of the time. Max looked up. "Did you take the picture out?"

"No. I was too in shock seeing him again. I didn't know what to think."

"I'm glad you hung onto it. I think this is our contact item. Do you have a hairpin? Something to pry out the picture?"

"Let me see." Deidre got up and went to the dressing table where she had laid out her things. "How about a brooch pin?"

"That will do. Bring it here."

She returned to where he sat on the bed and handed it to him. He released the pin and poked gently under the picture, trying to pry it out. It popped out easily, landing on the floor. Max stood and picked it up. "There's writing on the back."

"What does it say?"

"Amersham Market, 1928."

They looked at each other for a moment. Max was the first to speak. "The rendezvous is in the future."

"Looks that way. Can I have the locket back?"

Max leaned toward her and caressed her face before reaching back to clasp the claw to the chain. "There. Keep it safe. I've memorized it. Best way to store important information." He tapped his head.

She looked up at him. He was so close she could feel his body heat, even through the many layers of their Edwardian wardrobes. He slipped his hands from her neck, down her back, to her waist. She moved her hands under his jacket, feeling the sculpted definition of his chest through his shirt. Feeling him so close, she didn't know if she wanted to stop. Her head was in a muddle.

He broke the silence. "We're going to need to charge our bracelets."

"I know." Her breath came out rushed. "I'd rather with you."

He cupped her face in both hands. "I know this is confusing, and I'm not sure how this will turn out."

"And having James alive again isn't changing how I feel now. It's confusing, I'll admit." She looked into his eyes. "But I still feel drawn to you. Like I want to explore these feelings between us. This attraction."

He reached down and took her hands in his. He kissed the tips. "I didn't want to tell you about James. I was afraid."

She put her fingertips to his lips. She traced the edges of his mouth as he closed his eyes. "Afraid I'd only want him?" She paused watching him enjoy her touch. "I am so glad you told me how you feel. Because I think I'm falling for you too."

He opened his eyes. Hope flared within them. "Too?"

"How do they say it in this time? I'm mad for you."

With that, he unleashed his eagerness on her lips. She opened up to him, her tongue exploring inward. Together, they danced with each other's mouths as their passion spilled to the rest of their bodies. They feverishly began removing their clothes. Each clamored with the buttons of the other.

"Damn Edwardians. They make everything harder." Max struggled with her jacket, taking a breath between kisses to speak.

"Why do all the little buttons have to be so far apart on men's shirts? I like the Velcro closures of our time." Deidre pulled at the bottom part of Max's shirt, popping buttons in all directions.

"Good idea." Max went to pull hard on Deidre's blouse and found it hard to pull open. "Your seamstress is too good."

She stood back and undid the rest of her buttons, tossing the blouse to the floor. Max stood before her, his shirt hanging open, gazing at her in her layers of undergarments.

"You're a feast for the eyes, Deidre."

"I have three more layers to remove before you get to feast on anything."

"And I am looking forward to removing them, one by one."

"I bet you say that to all of the ladies you court in this Edwardian Age."

"Stop the playing, Deidre." He stepped toward her and gently caressed her bare arms, "I love you. I want you more than anyone I've ever encountered. Playing with my heart is cruel."

"I'm not."

"I know your feelings for James are deep."

She grabbed his face in her hands. "James is dead to me, remember?" She took his mouth in hers. He gave himself to her. He let his hands drift over her the soft fabric over her breasts, just firmly enough for her nipples to react, then exploring lower. She felt her middle begin to melt, the heat driving her to pull off his shirt, exposing his shoulders. She kissed him along his collarbone, across his chest, and then down to his abdomen.

With a glance up to his face, she saw him looking down at her. She took that gaze as his approval for her to keep going. She undid his trousers and pushed them to the floor, releasing his eager and erect cock. Caressing down the soft skin, she kissed his sensitive tip. Licking the edge, she wrapped her lips around his shaft and took him fully in her mouth. Moans escaped him.

She looked up at him, smiling like the devil. "I do care for you. What comes of the rest, time will tell. For now, I want you."

"I am yours, my love," he whispered.

She rubbed down the back of his smooth shaft, feeling the back along the vein. She fingered his delicate sacks, listening for his moans again. She formed her mouth into an "O," and took him again deeply into her mouth. Slowly gliding her lips over his soft skin, she took him fully again. Then, she teasingly backed away. He reached for her head, curling her hair around his fingers. "My God, Deidre. I never imagined you would do this to me."

She responded to his enthusiasm by moving faster and faster, stopping around his man's head to lick him into a frenzy. His moans answered her. She kept to her rhythm, listening for his breathing as it grew heavy and rasped. "Oh God, Deidre."

She stopped and looked up. "Do you want me?"

He pulled her up from the floor and pushed her down on the bed. "I want you more than life itself."

"Prove it by taking me now."

There was quick break in the passion when he had to step out of his pants and took off his shoes, but then he returned his full attention to her. She too was taking a moment to free herself from her camisole. Pulling her skirts off, her laughter awakened more desire, and he dropped atop her, pinning her to the bed with his body. "What are you doing to me, woman?"

"Falling for you, Max."

"I've dreamed of this moment."

"Make it come true, Max." She winked at him.

He reached for her inner folds, finding the spot to give her the most pleasure. "You're already wet and ready for me."

"I told you. No foreplay." She settled into the pillows, smiling.

"I don't want to rush this." Easing over her he gently kissed her stomach, the small indention in her hips, which led him toward the inviting warmth of her inner thighs. With each kiss, he brought her body to the next level. Every nerve felt alive, every muscle pulled taut like an archer's bow.

"Max, you devilish man."

"You said you wanted to be taken like I take all my Edwardian women. I need to appreciate the womanly form."

"You're such a romantic."

"I am." He leaned over her naked body, their scents mixing with their sweat. "I want to take all of you a little at a time. There is so much about you I want to appreciate." He kissed her, nipping at her lower lip. I relish every piece of you."

"I want to see what you can bring out of me." She held his face. "Teach me about love."

Her words spurred him into a frenzy, and he reached to find her intimate opening. He let his fingers rest a moment on her warm, moist lips and felt her own hand cover his as she encouraged his finger inside. He responded, thrusting his finger deep within, bringing a surge of wetness. Rubbing her nub with his thumb, he heard her gasp. She opened her legs wider to allow him full access. He whispered to her. "Tell me. What do you want from me?"

"Love me, Max."

He looked into her eyes, balancing over her, seeking her wet folds with his cock. He rubbed the opening.

"Don't torture me, Max. I want you deep in me."

He kissed her, pushing into her slowly as their hips moved to conform to each other. With a hard thrust, he took her. Their gasps matched with each push. "Say it again."

"I want you, Max."

He drove deep, her head arching back. "Do you love me, Deidre?"

"Yes," she said.

He thrust deep within her again and again. She leaned up, raising her hips to lock them together in an intimate embrace. Her head bent back in the pillows. The rising tide built in her, the crest of love building to a peak. Her heart beat faster and faster, her mind forgetting everyone but Max. Deep within, she felt the emotions build and break, and she shouted, "I love you, Max."

He thrust one last time. Her cry met his as they climaxed together, breathing and panting their love to its finish. The dings from their bracelets told them the energy had been stored.

Max collapsed on Deidre, pinning her safely below him. He looked as if she'd slain him. "I'm utterly yours, Deidre."

She looked at him, holding his gaze and reaching her leg around him to keep him close. "I'm yours too. Partners, my love. Until the end."

Untangling his limbs from Deidre, Max slid out of bed, disturbing Deidre's sleep.

"Don't go." She sat up and watched him put on his trousers, admiring his naked torso as she recalled how tasty it had been, each kiss a bit salty with his sweat.

"I have to. We can't be seen like this. It's not what sisters and brothers do." He winked at her. He finished fastening his trousers and walked over to the bed, crushing her back into the thick down comforter as he fell back on top of her. "Though, I'd stay if I could. You know that."

"I know." She kissed him. "You're right. This would be something very hard to explain. But I'm sure we'll have to charge the crystals at least two more times before we can make the next jump."

He pulled away and looked into her eyes. There was no mischief there. "This was more than a crystal charge."

"Yes. It was." She kissed him again, and then pushed him gently. "But we can't risk you staying."

"I know. We've got to finish this mission to appease the Council."

She rolled over toward him and rested her chin on his shoulder. "Then, we jump to meet James."

He gave her a squeeze then sat up and reached for his shoes. "Yes." There was a moment when neither of them spoke.

"I just can't believe he's alive. It's hard to fathom," Deidre finally said.

He finished fastening his shoes and looked over at her. "Really? I haven't wiped him from your mind." He gave her a bittersweet smile.

"You're helping now." She rolled onto her stomach, propping her hands under her chin to watch him.

"Let's not talk of him unless we have to. Agreed?"

"Right." She watched him finish with his clothes as she lay on her stomach, her naked body on display for him, in a pose just like those old posters of brazen women of the time. Her legs bent, with her feet swinging coquettishly as she watched.

He turned. "You're making it really hard to leave, especially when you pose like that."

"Who me?" She pointed to her naked breast demurely. "Really, I'm just lying here."

"Exactly." Fully dressed, he leaned down to kiss her. "I better go now before I take you again."

She rolled off the bed, slinking her naked body to his side. "Soon, I hope."

"We may need adjoining rooms if we stay here for a long time."

"You like the idea of staying?" She leaned against him, brushing him with her naked breasts.

He grabbed her around the waist. "Yes. It could work until we have to make the jump. We wouldn't need to go back and forth to London. You could finish studying Henri, and we could do the jump from here."

Her hands moved up his back to wrap around his neck. "Sounds like a plan."

"Damn it." He kissed her again, lingering on her lips. "I have to leave. This time, before I change my mind." He let her go, turning to look at her one more time. She bent her leg at an angle, sidled her hips, and put her hands at her sides. He shook his head. "You are Venus incarnate, Deidre."

"Maybe Henri will make me his next statue subject?"

"Don't you dare. That would be too dangerous."

"It's how I usually get my best information. I'm very good at posing nude."

He shook his head. "I bet you are." He blew a kiss. "I've got to go. Until tomorrow, sister dear."

She sat on the bed as he opened the door. "Good night, brother dear."

Max slowly closed the door and started to walk down the hall. As he proceeded to his room, a door opened and Henri peeked out. "Is Deidre all right, Max?" He blinked his eyes several times. His nose was red. Sleep still clung to him.

"Yes. I checked on her. She is going to sleep. I had some family news to give her, and it seemed quite upsetting to her."

Henri stepped out into the hall. "That's why you had to speak to her so late, I presume."

"Yes. It was quite sudden. If you'd excuse me, I'm retiring for the evening. Good night to you, Henri."

"Good night." Henri watched Max carry on down the corridor. He turned and returned to his room. Closing his door, he thought about checking on Deidre in the morning. He intended to make her his own. Tomorrow, he might make her a proposition.

Fifteen

Henri walked down the hall to Deidre's door. Standing in front of it, he hesitated to knock. Would she be awake this early? He bolstered himself, taking a deep breath, and knocked.

From inside, Deidre called, "Who's there?"

"Henri. I met your brother in the hall last night. He said you've received bad news from home. Do you need assistance?"

"Just a moment." There was some rustling and noise from inside, and then Deidre opened the door, standing with her hands holding her silk robe closed. "Come in, Henri."

Henri entered and looked around. His eyes rested on her clothes lying on one of the chairs, and the tousled sheets of the bed. "What have you been doing here?"

"What do you mean?"

"I heard a lot of moaning and moving around in here last night."

"Oh, my brother was just counseling me. It was very upsetting news from home. A shock really. You must have heard me crying last night."

Henri perked up with this. "Crying? My dear Deidre, it's not so distressing is it?" He came forward and put his hand on her face, stroking her cheek.

"Yes. Well, all this talk of my late husband James and now with the news from home, it was a trying evening."

He lowered his hand. "He was your late husband? Oh my dear Deidre, it must be crushing to share your loss with our little group." His dark hair flopped into his eyes. His brown eyes sparkled as they had in the garden.

She took his hand. "Yes. Especially in times such as this, when I feel so alone without him." She looked up at him, letting her eyes grow wide. "Do you know what it's like to be alone?" She left her lips parted, hoping for Henri's sweet kiss again. Damn what Max said. She'd be careful.

"Yes, I do." He bent down, meeting her lips, joining in a gentle touch.

Deidre pulled back first. "Henri, my brother is wary that we should be together. I must be careful."

"He seems to be over protective of you."

"He is my older brother."

"I know I'd want to protect you from other men. It's not hard to imagine."

She moved her hand to his chest, tracing up the center of the material. "There is something you could do for me."

He grabbed her hand. "What is that, my love?"

"Could I be your subject? It's my dream to be the subject of a masterpiece." She backed up looking him eye to eye. "I've been thinking of the pose I might do. Can I show you?"

Henri let go of her hand, and lowered himself to sit on the bed, clearing his throat. "Of course."

"You are a strict professional." Henri nodded as she went on. "Then, I want you to give me your opinion. In the strictest professional degree."

"Yes."

"Tell me if I would make a good subject." She opened her robe and dropped it to the floor. Her naked body was in its full glory before him. Henri cleared his throat again. She lowered herself to the small love seat against the wall, lying upon it, draping her limbs over the edges. "Would you be able to make something artistic out of my form?"

"You are a goddess, Deidre." His eyes were wide looking up and down her length. "Your body sings its form to me. I would make you my Aphrodite."

"I'm glad to hear it." She reached down and picked up her robe. Standing, she placed it back around her shoulders and wrapped the cord to fasten it closed. "I wanted to practice some poses to see what would work best. I've always fantasized about posing for a sculptor. Could you make my fantasy come true, Henri?" She reached her hands around his shoulders, gliding them up behind his neck. "Make my fantasy come true, Henri." She brushed her lips against his.

"I would be honored to sculpt you, my dear." He bent his face down to hers, kissing her again. They came closer in their embrace, and Henri pulled back. Fully flushed, he said, "I will need to make arrangements for you to pose. But we can do that later today." His voice cracked a bit. "I think I should meet you later downstairs, and let you get ready for the day."

"Of course, Henri dear."

His voice held a rasp as he cleared it again. "I will see you down at breakfast after you dress, my dear." He turned and moved to the door, opening and closing it as if in a great escape.

Deidre laughed, clapped her hands, and fell on the bed. "I cannot wait." Her laughter was loud enough for Henri to hear as he hurried down the hall to his door. He looked back for just a moment before entering the safety of his room.

"Are you sure you don't want to travel back with me?" Max stood in front of Deidre. He held her hands while the driver was loading his trunk into the carriage.

"I really should stay here. If I can finish the mission, then we might be able to fix the timeline and appease the Time Council faster." She squeezed his hands. "It will only be a few days until you return. I'll be fine here." She kissed his cheek and whispered in his ear. "I've gotten Henri to request I pose for him. I'll get close enough to study his technique."

He looked her up and down. She caught the hardness in his eyes. Was it jealousy? She was sure he was mulling it over. "Fine. Stay. We need to sort out our standing with the Council. It might work if we still played by their rules." He leaned closer and whispered, "Do be careful. Remember, don't get too close."

She held his hand. "Travel safely, brother dear." She let him go and went to gather her skirt to step off the carriage step.

Max took a moment to look at his pocket watch, holding the door open. "Give my regards to everyone. I'll be back in a few days."

"Wait."

Deidre turned her head to get a better look at who was shouting. Henri was raising his hand, shouting, racing down the stairs of the entry of the main house to their carriage.

"Wait. Please wait." Henri stopped by them, breathing heavily. "Where are you both going?"

"Max is going to get our things from the inn." She looked up to see Max leaning out of the window, looking down at them both.

"What's up, ole boy?" Max smiled down at Henri.

"Well then." Henri moved forward, reaching for Deidre's waist. "She'll be fine here while you fetch everything. I'll make sure she's properly cared for." He pulled her his direction. Deidre slid up next to Henri and wrapped her arm around his waist.

Max crossed his arms looking them both over. "Are you certain you'll be all right?" He raised an eyebrow in concern. "I'm not sure how you'll get along without me," he added, trying for levity.

"I've been traveling around a good portion of Europe before you arrived," Deidre answered. "Don't worry. Hurry back, though. I'll need your advice on my...poetry." She waved at him, covering her mouth from Henri's view as she worded with her lips, *the mission.*

"Are you sure?" He eyed Henri's arm wrapped around Deidre's waist.

"Yes. I might make some progress on that poem I was talking about with you last night."

Henri grabbed Deidre's hands. "And please know, if you have any more of that pressing family business, you can feel free to attend to it, knowing your sister is in good hands." He started to guide her back to the main house.

She looked up to Henri as they began to walk away. "Yes. It was upsetting to hear all of what is happening." She stopped and turned back to Max. "Do send a message home for me. It will do their hearts good to know our whereabouts."

Max sighed. "Fine. I'll fly like the wind back to London and return in a few days."

He leaned back and positioned himself in the seat. He shouted before closing the door and driving off. "You take care of her, Henri."

Henri turned and said, "I will." Still holding onto Deidre's waist, they both waved as the carriage rounded the drive and headed toward the gate. Deidre watched Max's face until he was out of sight. She could tell he was anxious and looked rather annoyed. She couldn't help it though. She had to do what research she could. If she stayed, she'd have a much better chance. Making sure Henri wanted her to stay was a step in the right direction.

She turned to him. "Thank you."

"For what?"

"I was trying to find a way to stay. You know my brother is awfully protective."

"I won't let anything happen to my little Deidre." He pulled her close and kissed the top of her head.

"I know you won't." She tried not to roll her eyes. She hated this age since they treated women like mere children. She did think it would be a way to get closer to him without getting too close. She could act more childlike, and the falsehood would keep them at a distance. She looked at him, pouting, and put her hands in his pockets. "My hands are cold."

Suddenly, a terrible feeling of déjà vu came over her. She stopped and turned to look at the carriage going down the drive. Her hands came to her mouth. She stood frozen.

"Deidre, what is it?" Henri reached for her, putting his hands on her arms as she stood as a statue.

The feeling didn't go away. It got more intense as the carriage she'd traveled in with James flashed in her mind, superimposing over the carriage holding Max. "Wait." She started to run, cursing the tight skirt of the age. "Wait." She tried waving her arms, but Max wasn't looking and obviously couldn't hear her. The carriage continued through the gate and turned onto the road.

Henri came running up behind her. "Deidre, what is it? Did you see something?"

"I just have a horrible feeling; I should have gone with him."

"What do you mean?" He rested a hand gently on her arm.

She stood looking toward the front gate. "I don't know. Maybe it's nothing." She tried to shake the feeling, but cold crept through her, giving her a feeling of unease. She wrapped her arms around herself to protect her from a spectral breeze.

Henri wrapped his arm around her shoulder and guided her toward the house. "Come. Let's go inside. Max would be upset if you got a chill. I promised I would take care of you."

"But it was like the last time."

"What last time?"

"With—" she stopped for a moment, remembering James getting into their carriage and leaving to take care of part of their mission. She had been with James that time. "My husband. He died in a carriage robbery."

"It's the trauma. Let's get you inside." He pulled her arm under his and helped her up the front steps. "It's almost time for lunch. We can have a bite, and then see what we can do about having you inspire my next sculpture."

This brought Deidre out of her dark mood. "Oh really? I can pose for you so soon?"

"Yes. You're my muse."

As they walked back to the house, she rested her head on his shoulder. But she still couldn't shake the feeling of foreboding. It wrapped around her heart, freezing it with a shadow.

It had been several days since Max had left. Deidre had kept busy posing for Henri and sharing poetry at night. Today, she lay on the divan, head back, a soft, sheer fabric draped across her body. Henri came over to adjust the fabric, moving it to one side and then to the other. She sighed. "How much longer?"

"I'm almost done getting the basic outline of your curves, darling."

"Fine, then. Is it all right if I close my eyes?"

"Yes. Just keep your arms and legs the way I placed them."

She didn't know what was wrong with her. She usually enjoyed posing. But Henri wasn't doing much but briefly touching her in the readjustments of the drape. He wasn't responding well to her looks. She eyed him slowly looking at her.

She rearranged her body so a corner of the fabric fell away, revealing part of her breast. Henri's eyes moved slightly. She waited a few moments for him to get back to his rough model that he was making. She loved to watch the movement of his hands, wondering if he was ever going to start using them on her.

She moved her hip slightly. The sheer fabric fell again. This time, completely exposing her left breast. Henri looked up and sighed. "Deidre, you moved?"

"Sorry." She pouted a little as he came over to adjust the fabric. She arched her back to wiggle her breast, slapping his hand playfully. Her nipple hardened at the connection. "Is it my imagination, or is it getting cold in here?"

He placed the drape back across her breast, tucking it slightly under her flesh. "Please try not to move."

"I promise."

Her evil grin made Henri frown. "Somehow, I think you might be doing this on purpose.""Do I have to wear the drape? Venus doesn't. You're being so English."

"It's not your body I'm trying to capture, but the mood."

"Then, it wouldn't matter if anything was exposed. I'm trying to sacrifice myself for art."

"Very well."

She let the drape fall to expose her breast again.

"You win. But don't move anymore. I know you want to sacrifice for art, but it isn't necessary for you to corrupt yourself."

"I am not corruptible, Henri." She parted her lips, licking them slightly. "I'm your Aphrodite, remember?"

"Yes." He turned and went back to the mound of clay he was turning into the prototype model. "Please don't move for just a little longer."

"And then what?" She put a sultry whisper in her voice.

He stopped working the clay and looked at her. "What do you mean?"

"What would you like to do to me after you're done?" She fluttered her eyelashes. "I long for your kisses, Henri."

"Try not to talk. If you distract me, I won't be able to finish."

"If I move, you'll do what?"

He stopped and put down his tools. "I want to ravish you in that position. That's what I'm trying to capture. If you keep at me, I don't know if I can keep my resolve."

"Oh. I see. I'll hold still, if you promise to ravish me when you're done."

"Yes." He sighed, and then she saw his brown eyes sparkle as he looked at her. "Are you always this difficult?"

"My brother says I am."

"I wouldn't be surprised. Now stay still."

She didn't answer, but put her lips together in a provocative look toward Henri. She felt her nipples harden as she concentrated on him. His brown hair fell in his eyes as he produced a likeness of her form in the clay. Her pose was transformed into the clay by his fingers. She watched him mold and caress the lump that was forming. She appeared to be standing as opposed to lying down, but that was the only difference. He knew if she posed standing for a long time, it would have been too hard for her. She was thankful. It was hard lying down this long. To have stood up to pose would have been a burden.

What seemed like another hour went by. Deidre was starting to fall asleep. Her arm slowly slipped off the divan where she'd rested it behind her head. It returned her to full consciousness. "Henri. I'm sorry. I think I'm falling asleep."

She looked over to where he had been seated by the prototype clay model. He wasn't there. She sat up, this time pulling the sheer fabric up around her. It was starting to get very cold in the studio. She got up and walked over to see Henri's prototype.

The mound of clay was in her form, with her arms folded back and her legs showing. Surprisingly, he'd added her breast forms, but they were the hint of the shape. Her head looked like it was from an ancient statue; her hair in a solid ancient wig. The fabric draped around her legs hid her most private parts. It was the makings of a great piece of art. In fact, she remembered it being in the pictures of art in her report on Henri before she jumped to London.

She wrapped the drape around her more tightly and smiled. "I'm officially art now." She hadn't seen herself immortalized before.

She felt him come up behind her. "Yes, you are, and you're beautiful."

She turned to wrap her arms around his neck. "Thank you, Henri."

"You're very welcome."

"So, is it time to ravish me now?"

He answered by pressing his lips against hers. She nibbled at his lower lip, sneaking her tongue into his mouth, reaching deeply, exploring. He pulled her closer, and her fabric barrier fell to the floor. She pressed her breasts up against him. He reached down and grabbed her ass.

She slipped a finger under one of his suspenders, and pulled it off his shoulder. It fell to his hip. She did the same with the other one. Slowly, she unbuttoned his shirt and reached under the cotton fabric to caress his chest, feeling his own goose bumps of anticipation.

Suddenly, Henri stopped kissing. He grabbed the loop of one of his suspenders and tried to place it back on his shoulder. "Stop, Deidre. We can't. We've got to stop."

"Why?" Her hands remained on his chest, feeling the hammering of his heart beneath them.

"If we continue like this, I'm afraid that we'll end up doing something indecent."

She whispered, "That's what I'm hoping."

"How could you want that? I don't want to ruin you."

"You won't, Henri. You don't know me very well, you know."

"That's the other reason. No." He took her hands and pulled them out from under his shirt. "We have to stop. I don't want to take you this way."

"What way do you want to take me?"

"Deidre, you're making it very hard to act like a gentleman." He held her hands and kissed the tips. "I assure you, I want you very much. But we have to wait for the right time."

"All right." She bent and picked up the sheer fabric, wrapping it around herself again, though certainly not for modesty's sake. "I understand." She couldn't help the pout that was forming. "Are you sure?" She eyed him again.

"Yes. Absolutely. I promised your brother I'd take care of you. I'm sure this isn't what he had in mind."

"How do you know?" She smiled, coming up with an idea. "I am in Europe looking for a husband. You could be him." She leaned up against him, kissing him softly.

Brushing her lips back, he grabbed her hands again. "Then, if and when that time comes, we wait."

She leaned up and kissed him again. "All right. If and when." She shivered. "I think I should get dressed. I'm starting to get cold."

"All of your things are still behind the screen over there." He pointed over to the dressing screen. She stepped behind the screen and started to dress in the Edwardian brown and white pin-striped two-piece dress she had arrived in. She put her legs into the pantaloons, cinched up her corset, and eased her blouse over her head. She pulled on her skirt and slipped on her jacket completing her Edwardian outfit. After a long sigh, she came out from behind the screen. "Sorry I took so long."

"Not at all." Henri came forward and put a hand on either side of her waist. "Women take a while to get dressed. Never be ashamed of being a woman." He kissed her and straightened her neckline and jacket. "You're a very special woman, Deidre."

"How do you know?"

"It's what you do to me that tells me so."

A knock echoed through the studio. They both looked at each other. The knock happened again, echoing against the wooden door. Henri let Deidre go and walked over to the door, easing it open. Deidre heard muffled talk, followed by the full creak of the door. She spied Wyndham and John coming into the studio. Their faces looked stern and grim. Whatever happened wasn't good.

Wyndham asked, "Henri, have you seen Deidre?"

"I'm here." Deidre moved away from the screen and walked over to Henri. He wrapped his arm around her waist. "What is it?"

"Bad news, I'm afraid." John wrung his hands, looking at Deidre. "We've had news from London that your brother has been arrested for robbery."

"What?" Deidre's hands flew to her face. "What do you mean?"

Wyndham sounded dark. "We've also gotten a message to hold you too. As his accomplice."

"What are you talking about?" Henri's voice was ripe with rage.

",That they are not who they appear to be." John's voice joined Wyndham's in a powerful darkness. Something was very wrong.

"What are you implying?" Henri's voice rose with indignation.

Wyndham sighed, tiring of the exchange. "Simply that our dear Deidre is a thief." He turned to Deidre. "An inspector has arrived with a warrant saying you are a swindler along with your brother. Everything you've been telling us is a lie. We got it from the inspector himself. He's waiting to see you."

Deidre's face grew pale. Her feeling of something going wrong with Max had happened. "My brother's not a thief, and neither am I."

"The inspector is waiting, Deidre. You can explain it all to him." Wyndham's hand pointed to the door.

"Fine. I will." She flounced her skirt as she went out the door. She headed to the main house followed by the men. Henri followed quickly behind her. She looked back once and saw the worry in his eyes. She wasn't going to let hers show. This had to be a mistake.

Sixteen

"You've been accused of helping your brother steal from well-to-do families in France." The inspector had the thick, handlebar mustache with curls at the end. His rather plain brown suit fit his sullen face. His bowler seemed worn from use.

She stomped her foot in protest. "It's just not true. I don't know who is telling filthy lies about us, but we're here visiting from the States."

He didn't seem to be buying Deidre's denials. "Your brother is being taken to Scotland Yard to be questioned. They are going to want to send him back to Paris along with you."

"My father is going to be furious when he gets word of this." Deidre was trying to bluff. She knew this was bad. Whoever made up these charges was out to get them both. But who would do that?

"It's too late to go back to London now." The inspector looked at John. "If you wouldn't mind lodging myself and my prisoner."

"Of course." John nodded, completely slumping his shoulders.

Deidre didn't miss a beat. "PRISONER? What do you mean?"

"You'll have to go with him, Deidre, to sort this out," Wyndham said.

"But it's not true." Her voice went shrill.

Henri held her hand. "Until we know otherwise, you're going to have to go with him. I'll go with you if you like?"

Deidre's heavy breathing made it hard for her to speak. She sighed to control herself. "Yes, please, Henri. If you'll come with me, I'd feel much better." She raised her hand to his face.

"Yes, of course."

"Fine. We'll leave in the morning then." The inspector clasped his hands behind his back. "Until then, I'll have to ask that you lock the prisoner in her room."

"Must you call her that?" Henri exclaimed, reaching for Deidre's hands. "It's all right." He kissed her hands, looking at her. "We'll figure a way to get you and your brother free of these horrendous charges."

"Then, you believe me?"

"Of course, darling."

The inspector coughed loudly. "Would you be good enough to take us to her room? I want to supervise the locking of the young lady in her chamber. I want to make sure there is no funny business before we leave in the morning."

Henri answered, "I'll gladly escort her."

"Do I really have to be locked up?"

"It will be easier if we do as he says, Deidre." He patted her hand again.

She let Henri take her to her room, followed by the inspector who watched as Henri walked her inside. Henri gave her a small kiss on the cheek. "Try to get a good night's sleep, Deidre. You will need it for tomorrow's trip."

"I will. Thank you, Henri." She gave him a small peck of a kiss. She wanted to do more, but not in front of the watchful eyes of the inspector.

Deidre stood looking at the door, hearing the lock engage with a finite click. She rubbed her arms, feeling cold. What was she going to do? What had happened with Max? There had to be a way to figure this out.

She sat on the bed, wrapping her arms around her, trying to think through what could have happened. She wrangled her mind for an answer. Max must have gotten to the inn and encountered the police, or they stopped him at the train station. She wasn't sure about the details, but she was sure this was not a good spot to be in.

She walked to the window and looked outside. She was on the second floor. It was too high to jump out. She was definitely a prisoner. What could she do? She only had her time bracelet. She wasn't sure if she was in the range of her time vehicle to call it. But she could try.

She tried tapping the bracelet. It answered with a beep showing she was out of range. She should have known better than to leave it behind. She thought it was going to be a simple trip out to the country. It was turning into a disaster.

She paced around the room not knowing what to do with herself. She spotted a pitcher of water on the desk and poured herself a glass. Looking around, she tried to find some wine. Nothing. Damn. Not even alcohol to make her sleepy.

She lay down on the bed and tried to think clearly. If only there was some way to contact Max. She tried not to think of him in jail, in filthy hay with stale bread and water. She was better off at least. Thankfully, she didn't have rats scurrying around her feet.

It simply had to be a misunderstanding. Who would want to hurt them? Accuse them of being swindlers? She tried to get comfortable, but her mind was too full to get any rest. She wished that she knew where Max was. Whether he had gotten hurt when they captured him. She had no way to know what had happened on the road to London. She tried breathing in and out to steady her nerves. Tomorrow it would be all sorted. Henri would help explain. Unless there was something more to this.

What if the attacks weren't just attacks on her? There had to be something about the fact that Max had gone rogue. It couldn't be coincidence that suddenly law enforcement was being tipped off that they were criminals. Someone had to be behind it. Or something.

The thought froze her. What if the Time Council was behind everything? The attacks on her. The police trying to arrest them. They could easily plant facts into the past to help a timeanaut. What about facts to hinder them? She bit her lip. If the Time Council had that much power to affect them in the past, what else could it do? She was going to need to stick to her mission if they had any chance.

Her thoughts were interrupted by something striking the window. *Click. Click.* She turned toward it and heard it again. *Click.* Moving to the window, she saw a pebble hit the outside, making another clicking sound. Catching the latch, she unhooked it and looked down below her.

Standing below her window was Max. His clothes were disheveled. He had a sack next to him and waved to her. He cupped his hands. In a loud whisper, he said, "Take off all of your clothes except your pantaloons. Tie your sheets together and climb down. I've got clothes for you down here."

She whispered down. "Max, what happened?"

"I'll tell you once you're down here. Hurry. This is making too much noise."

Deidre sprang into action. She shed her layers of Edwardian dress, leaving only her pantaloons and blouse. She was relieved to be rid of the corset and heavy skirts. Whatever had happened, Max was sure to have a plan.

She grabbed her sheets and started tying them together. She ended up needing to use some strips of her heavy bedspread to make the right length. Tossing the makeshift rope out the window, she tied it to the bedpost. She hopped out and made her way down the side of the building. The rope stopped just shy of the ground.

Max whispered, "Let go. I'll catch you."

She let go and felt his arms catch her. They fell back into the dirt from the impact of her landing. She rolled on top of Max and kissed him.

His lips pushed back for a brief moment. "Not now. We've got to get out of here." He continued in a hushed voice. "I'll tell you everything. Head to the stables. I found some men's clothes for you."

They got up off the ground, brushed off quickly, and grabbed hands. They ran together to the stables. Max handed her the man's shirt, waistcoat, and pants. He even had some worker's boots for her near to her size.

She whispered, "Where did you get these?"

"Don't worry about that now. We've got to get out of here. They may be coming for you too."

"There's an inspector here already." She adjusted the belt to make the pants fit her waist. "They were going to take me to London in the morning."

"Then, at least we're in time to get out of here. Come on." Max grabbed her arm.

She took a look back at the main house. She tried to forget about Henri. "I guess finishing the mission isn't an option. The Council must be really pissed off."

"More than pissed off," answered Max. "I'd say they've targeted us for trial and termination. We're officially Time Rogues."

She gulped, looking away from the house. "Let's get out of here."

"It's just about fifteen miles from here, over by the Misbourne River. I remote called my time vehicle, and hid it in a field between the train station and the river. It ran out of power by then. It's near the market hall where James said to meet. Then, I came back to find you. We should be able to get there by tomorrow." Max's voice held the chance of hope in his tone.

They'd been keeping off the roads, but following along the train tracks to make it to the next village. They were passing through some of the fields outside of Great Missenden.

Deidre stopped for a moment to get her breath. "Any idea when we can stop? We've been walking most of the night."

Max looked around. "You're right. It's going to be light soon. We're going to have to find a place to hole up during the day. Let's keep going until we find something."

"I hope we find somewhere soon. I'm starting to lose my momentum."

"Wait. I think I see some sort of structure by that creek over there." Deidre looked to see where Max was pointing. Sure enough, there was a stone structure by the creek, surrounded by a few grazing sheep. The roof looked to be made out of thatch and sticks strung together. "If you don't mind sharing a space with sheep, it might do."

"I don't care as long as I can lie down somewhere. I'm asleep on my feet." They walked over to the pasture and came to the side of the building just along the small creek. The burble of the water was a welcome invitation. Deidre knelt down next to a rock and scooped up some of the cool liquid.

"You know we should boil that first." He stood next to her.

She stopped drinking for a moment. "My NaNoBots will keep the dysentery from happening." She scooped up another hand full. The water trickled between her fingers as she slurped.

"Okay. It's your insides that might regret it later." He bent down next to her. "But it won't stop some of the effects. It might not be a pleasant experience to have a stomach ache." She stopped drinking. Water fell down between her fingers. " But we can find some safer water a bit later. I don't think we have a choice now." She took another slurp from her hand. "Besides, it doesn't taste foul. It might have just been some recent rain water from the hills." She looked at him watching the water drip from her fingers. "We're going to have to drink sometime."

Max knelt down beside her and cupped some water in his hand. He slurped until he was satisfied. "You're right. This is good."

She licked her lips. "It's could be natural spring water too. Our water doesn't taste this good."

"Because it's mostly synthetic. We lost natural water production when the weather system was programmed over the planet. Remember your history?"

"Yes." She knelt down for another drink. "It's why I enjoy researching so much. The world is so different in the past." She didn't want to think about what had happened. That they were now Time Rogues. Most likely, she wouldn't be able to do research again. This time period could be her new home.

After a long drink each, they went to check out the small building. It turned out to be more like a hut, an overnight retreat or rain break for a shepherd. It would give them shelter during the day. On closer inspection the roof was made of straw, insulated with mud and grass. Hay was strewn about the floor, with a very large pile in one corner along with some blankets. Some pots and pans were stacked to the side, along with a satchel of potatoes and carrots. Deidre found a box as well.

"What do you think this is?" She held it up for Max to see.

"I think it's an actual tinder box. I've never seen one in person. Fabulous." He took it from her, slid the wooden top off, and took out the flint and steel. "See, you strike one against the other, and sparks fly off to start your fire. You need small kindling and then build from there."

"Good. We've got food and fire for later." She began to move the blanket over the hay to make a pallet. "Now, I've got to sleep awhile."

"I'll keep watch and join you in a bit." He took off his jacket and laid it over her. "I want to make sure no one can follow our trail."

When she awoke, the light had gotten brighter. Max was lying next to her, a blanket wrapped around him in the hay. Some bits had gotten stuck in his brown, wavy hair. She started to pick some out, looking at his beautiful sleeping face. She hadn't had much time to think about what would happen to Max when she met James again. She knew it felt like it was over with James, but she wasn't sure how she'd react when she saw him again.

He was dead, and now alive. Something she desperately wanted. But then she looked at Max's sleeping face again. She wanted to kiss him while he slept. She leaned down to brush her lips against his.

His eyes fluttered and then opened. He reached out to her face and pulled her toward him, kissing her deeply. She moved to curl her limbs around his. His heart beat against hers. They mashed the hay below them, making a rustling noise as they moved.

"So, tell me," she said, pulling away for a moment. "Do we have a plan?"

His arms wrapped around her back. "Yes."

"You going to fill me in?"

"Well, we've got to make it to the time vehicle first."

"Yes, and?"

"We've got to jump to the time to meet James."

At the mention of his name, she tensed in Max's arms and leaned closer. "We'll have to travel to... What was it called, Amersham Market? In 1928? That might take two more charges,

I think." She gave him a sultry look, envisioning the sex they'd have to achieve full power.

"True," he replied, seeming equally enthused. He grabbed Deidre, moving on top of her. "No better time than the present."

But then his mood shifted. "But we're going to be stuck in 1914 England, where we are wanted criminals, until we can get to the time vehicle and make the next jump."

"Max, I want you to know."

He leaned back for a moment. "Yes?"

"No matter what happens, I care about you now. I want you to be careful."

"I want you to be careful, too, my Deidre. I wanted to have more time with you before all of this blew up in my face. But we have the present."

He kissed her, and she shut off her mind from the future and the past. His touch kept her fully in the present as he slipped his hands under her man's shirt.

Unbuttoning her waistcoat, he found her breasts easily without all the Edwardian corset and frills to get in his way. "Now this is more like it."

Deidre was working fast to unbutton his shirt. "No kidding. I'm definitely glad to be out of those dresses."

Though on the run, their foreplay was not as frenzied as it had been that first night they were together. Each of them seemed to want to take it slowly. Easily. She finished unbuttoning his shirt and caressed his defined chest, looking up into his warm eyes. "I was so worried what had happened to you, Max. They said you were in jail."

"I was. I was taken to the local jail, and they were readying to take me to Scotland Yard for questioning when I managed to take out my two guards." He answered her between kisses. "They had billy clubs, but they weren't a match for a trained timeanaut." He kissed down her throat to her breasts. Moving aside her shirt, he fondled her breasts, tweaking her nipples. "I missed these. These—and your safety, of course—were all I could think of as I made my way back to the manor house. I knew I had to get to you before they did."

"Who do you think they are?" She leaned her head against the hay.

He returned to kissing her neck. "I'm guessing the Council has sent more agents after us. We've broken timeanaut law and gone against the Council. Our lives will be forfeited to save the timeline."

"You didn't have to do this, Max." She held his attention, looking deep into his eyes.

"Yes I did. I would have died without you."

Deidre held him as he worked his way kissing under her chin. She felt his kisses travel down the side of her neck, but her mind wouldn't rest. She was too scared for them both. "Won't your time vehicle have its tracker on?"

"I dismantled it before I hid it." He looked up and tapped his head. "I was thinking ahead. If I managed to save you, I knew there would be trouble."

Still holding him, she said, "I'm glad you did. We're in this together."

"Yes." He stopped to look at her. "We are."

He started moving down her chest, sucking each nipple as he passed, then brushed her belly with his tongue. Deidre leaned back, her eyes rolling back in her head as she felt him undoing her trousers. He moved them down and stopped. "Pantaloons?"

She bit her bottom lip and opened her eyes wide. "You told me to wear them out the window, remember?"

He rubbed his nose against hers, grabbing the edge of her pantaloons. "It's the only thing that really speaks to a man in this age that he is about to take a woman. Removing her pantaloons." He gave an easy smirk and continued to slip them off, admiring her legs along the way. Then he pulled off his trousers, exposing his full need.

She wrapped her arms around his neck. "I've always wanted to be taken on a hay stack."

"It's rather rustic. You want to be taken rough?"

"No. Please. Take me gently, Max." She whispered in a raspy voice. "I want to remember every moment with you now. We don't know what the future holds. This could be…"

"Don't say it." He put his fingers to her lips. "I know. As rogues, there is no plan. There will be no record unless we want there to be one. We are masters of our own timeline now. Let's make one together."

"I'm scared of the future, Max."

"Don't be. I'm in it with you."

Max kissed her deeply, pulling on her lips like salvation as he reached for Deidre's lower regions. He parted her wet labia and slowly teased his way to her nub, already pulsing with excitement. He flicked and squeezed her, building her pleasure, and then slipped his finger deep within her, multiplying her pleasure. Again and again, he fingered her hard, until she couldn't take it. Waves of pleasure crested through her. She felt the shudder of her final release as he moved over her, kissing her nipples and chest.

"I've loved you for so long, Deidre. This is a waking dream for me." He kissed along her body, whispering against her skin.

"I knew this could happen. Defying the Council has its consequences. If this is my reward, I could die now as long as you still lived."

She kissed him, pulling him closer and feeling the muscles in his back. His eyes poured the passion he felt into her being. She felt her heart pound faster, needing him to unite them in the intimate embrace.

Straddling him, Deidre brought his manhood to her wet opening, moving against her moist lips. Teasing the entry, he felt the shocks of contact with her skin building him to thrust up into her. She began to ride him, up and down in a rocking rhythm, uniting them with each thrust.

She reached toward him. "Come inside me, my love."

He thrust into her, harder and harder, the shock sending her to throw her head back as she held him between her legs. Her muscles contracted around his cock, sending him near the edge. He pushed his hips to do a final thrust into her. Deidre joined him at the same time, the feelings traveling through her, breaking her body into shards. The pressure of her muscles around his cock released him into ecstasy. They came together, their breaths and hearts in rhythm. The only noise was their heavy breathing. She grabbed him close and looked into his eyes.

He kissed her and she moved to his side. "Don't worry. We'll get out of this. You trust me?"

"Yes." She put her hand on his chest. "Max?"

"Yes, my love." He lay next to her, his breathing still rapid.

"Do that to me again."

"When I reload. I think you've worn me out."

They lay in their shepherd's hut, listening to the sounds of the morning. Birds chirped outside the door. Max squeezed her tight. "Together." He whispered the word as she felt herself drift off to sleep again.

They awoke a few hours later, hay sticking out of their hair and stuck to their damp skin. "Here, I'll help get some of that out." Deidre brushed Max's chest free of hay.

"There's only one way to tackle this, I'm afraid." Max gave her a serious look.

"What do you mean?" Realization dawned on her face. "Oh no. You don't mean the creek?"

"A bath will wake us up."

"It's probably freezing."

"Do you want hay stuck to you all day?"

"No really. It's fine."

"Come on, it will be fun. There was a pond down on the other side of the building. Let's see how deep it is." He grabbed her hand and got her to stand up.

She didn't move, but rubbed her eyes and stretched. "You weren't kidding about loving going rustic."

"You're getting soft for a timeanaut, Deidre. Where's your sense of adventure?"

"But outside water?"

"You've never bathed in a pond?"

"No. Or waded. Or swam in a lake." She looked up at him, feeling like a schoolgirl. "I've read about them."

Max laughed. "Come on. I'll show you how."

Deidre shrugged her shoulders reluctantly, acquiescing. They slipped on their shirts and pants, carrying their boots, and headed toward the pond. When she saw the bugs flitting about the edge of the pond, she pulled back a bit. "They won't bite us, will they?"

"They're just dragon flies, Deidre. But I wouldn't catch one. I tried once. It bit me." He set down his boots and started taking off his shirt and trousers.

She stared a long time at the flying insects. One landed on one of the tall grasses growing at the edge of the pond. Its wings glinted in the afternoon sun. "If I'm not scared of racing through time, I can't be scared of you." The dragonfly sat, its legs holding onto the stalk. The sun gave its wings a rainbow shine. Its little head turned looking at her. "I can't be scared of such a beautiful thing."

She turned to see that Max had taken off his clothes and was walking toward her, stark naked. "Well, look at you!"

"How else does one take a bath, but in the nude?"

"I don't know, but I hadn't intended to strip by the side of the pond."

He spun around waving his arms. "There's nobody here. No one will see anything but me. And the sheep, of course."

"You're a man. It's easy for you. You can practically go naked at any time."

"Not any time." He walked forward, his hands easing around her waist. "If this were a public square, I wouldn't try."

"Point taken."

"Are you stalling?" His eyebrows rose to taunt her.

"No. Not at all." She set her boots down on a rock at the pond's edge and backed away from him, unbuttoning her shirt. She arched her back as she pulled her arms free, letting her breasts get a reaction. She wasn't disappointed. His shaft was on the rise in all its glory. She placed her shirt next to her boots, then took off her trousers, leaving her standing in just her pantaloons.

She slowly pulled them down, then turned and shook her bare ass at him as she tossed her pantaloons on the rock and went splashing into the pond. She let out a high-pitched squeal when she felt the water hit her skin. She didn't turn until she was submerged to her neck. Treading water, she shouted back. "Your turn."

As he approached the water, she couldn't help but notice his toned body. His well-formed muscular angles drew her eye. "You should be a model for the next sculptor."

He winced as he waded into the cold water. "I don't know if that will happen now. We're rogues, remember?"

"Sorry. It's going to take some getting used to. I'm so used to having a mission."

He quickly made the full-body plunge and swam toward her. "Something we'll both need to get used to. But I'd gladly do it again to save you." He found the pond floor and stood, wrapping his arms around her.

"What's our mission now?" She realized she could touch bottom, too.

"To get to James. He'll fill us in."

"About what?"

He pulled her closer. "To find out what has happened in the new timeline. Things have definitely changed. You're both alive, and time agents are after us. I imagine they might come for him too. It might be the three of us against the whole Time Council now."

"I'm not liking those odds."

"Could be worse."

"Like what?"

"You could be dead."

She nodded. "Point taken. The mission's over. Or is it? James was dead. This whole going back and saving me. You did it. So, being dead isn't permanent."

"I guess if you look at it that way, it might not be in some cases."

"Exactly." She put her hands on his chest. Looking up, she asked, "So if it had been reversed, if James had died, you wouldn't help him?"

"I can't say I would have known to. It was that way until you reached this assignment. This jump changed everything."

"It's changing me in more ways than I thought." Her lips touched his and they were lost in each other's kiss. Until they heard someone shout, "Hey, what's going on over there?"

They looked over to see an old man standing next to a woolly dog. He held a large rifle and was pointing the barrel toward them. His flat hat was over his eyes, and his stubble partially hid a wrinkled face. "How 'bout you both come out slowly?"

Max put his hands up immediately. "Please, don't shoot."

Deidre watched the dog, who looked not at all bothered by the humans. Its tongue lolled out as it panted. She sized up the situation quickly. "Please, sir. We only stopped to rinse off for a moment. We're just traveling through here."

"How do I know that for sure?" He kept the barrel leveled at them.

"You have my word." Keeping his hands raised, Max moved slightly forward. "This is my wife. She'll need to get out and dress proper. Please, I ask you. Let us get out and dress. We can talk once we are decent."

He seemed to assess their predicament. Lowering the gun, he turned to talk to the dog. "What do you say, Rusty?" The dog looked at him, and then at Max and Deidre. After a few sniffs, the dog looked back at the man and decided to lie down.

"Looks like it's settled. Rusty isn't worried about ya. Nor am I."

"Thank you, kind sir," Deidre said.

Max added, "It won't take us but a moment."

"I'll be in the shed. Make your way around when you're done."

They watched the man walk back to the small stone building. Slowly, they waded out of the water and started to dress.

"You think he's the shepherd that owns this place?" Deidre asked as she slipped her arms into her shirt.

"Must be. Glad he didn't find us asleep in there. At the least, we look like we took a stop in our travels."

"And not shagged each other silly, I hope." There was a glint in Deidre's eye when she put on her pantaloons.

"Not sure what he'll think."

"Why didn't you say I was a man?"

"From far away you can pass for it. But up close and personal, you are all woman in a man's clothes."

"What story should we tell him?"

"I'll think of something. Follow my lead." He finished buttoning his shirt, sat on a rock to slide on his boots, then stood and walked toward the shed. Deidre finished fastening her boots and followed.

They walked in to see the man had started a fire. He was sitting on an old stump that had been in the corner. He was cutting up potatoes and throwing them into a pot. "Come on in. I'm making lunch. Would you like some?"

"Yes. Very much." Deidre put on her simpleton face. "What's your name?"

"Burt. Burt Hesson. Where you two come from?"

"Up north," Max answered. "We've fallen on hard times and came south looking for work."

"I was wondering about your clothes." He looked over to Deidre, then back to Max. "Why does your wife dress like a lad?"

Deidre jumped in to answer for herself. "Dressing this way makes it easier to get work. Man's work suits me fine and pays more."

He took a long look at her, stopping for a moment from his cutting. "I could use some help around here. I'll trade a meal for some chores."

Max nodded. "Sounds fair." He put out his hand. "I'm Mark. This is my wife Dee."

Burt stood up and shook hands firmly. "Nice to know you both. I could use some help with the meal. In fact, if you took over Dee, I'd appreciate it. Then, I could show your husband a fence that needs mending."

Deidre walked over and took the potato and knife. "I'd be happy to." She took a seat on the stump as Burt waved to Max and walked toward the door. "Follow me. I'll show you what I mean."

Max looked behind him for a moment. Deidre waved him away. "Go ahead. I'll be fine here. When you both come back, I'll have a nice meal ready."

Burt led Max to a trail back along the creek. "I was wondering how I was going to get all this done before the next storm. I think some greater force has sent you to me for just that purpose."

They took another turn, following the creek that doubled back into the woods.

"I'm sure there is." Max smiled at him. "We are very grateful to you for helping us out."

"People like us have got to stick together." Burt slapped Max's back as they walked.

"Yes. We do."

"Where was it you said you were from?"

"North."

"Where up north?"

"Near Manchester."

"Really?" Burt stopped for a moment. He rubbed his chin. "Which town? My sister lives up there."

"Just outside of Manchester."

"You mean maybe near Salford?"

"Yes. Close by. Just south, near Trafford. Things are starting to get worse there, I'm afraid. Too many people have been losing jobs. We had to find a better place to work."

"Sorry to hear that. My sister married a man from the north. Good hard worker. I see you're a worker too." When they got to the edge of the woods, Burt stopped alongside a crumbled stone fence. "Let's get started in building this back up. I keep losing too many sheep to the woods."

They spent an hour building the wall back up. When Burt seemed satisfied, he patted Max on the back. "I think that will do for now. Let's head back and see what your wife has fixed up for us."

They headed back along the trail. Max was starting to take a liking to Burt. He was a pretty easy character, but he had one question on his mind. "Burt, I've been meaning to ask, why are you out here by yourself and not with your family?"

"My wife and I settled this land. We only had one daughter, a girl. She died from the consumption right when she was old enough to marry. My wife seemed to never be the same after that. But we carried on through the years together. She died last year."

"I'm so sorry to hear that." Max felt a lump rise in his throat. "I don't know what would happen if I lost Dee."

"Hold onto her tight, Mark. I don't regret any of the years I spent with Peg. She was a dear one. Always had a smile on her face, and a comment about her day to make me laugh." He looked down at the trail as they walked. "I miss her every day."

A silence hung between them as they walked along. When they neared the shed, they could both smell a vegetable stew on the breeze. Burt took a deep sniff. "Good to be coming back from morning work to smell something cooking from the shed again. Peg used to come up here and help me out from time to time while I watched over the sheep."

They walked in to see Deidre standing by the pot, the smell of fresh stew filling the shed. "Just about ready. Burt, I found a sack of vegetables with the potatoes. But I could only find two bowls and two spoons."

"Just my wife and me used this place. Since she died, I've been coming here only to check the sheep, but keeping a stock just for old times. It makes me think of her."

Deidre looked over at Burt. Her eyebrows lowered. "I'm sorry to hear about your wife. I'm sure she was a lovely lady."

"My Peg. She was the greatest." He changed the subject quickly. "But she wouldn't want guests to wait. How 'bout you both eat first. I'll share a bowl with the first done."

Deidre smiled as she spooned stew into the two bowls, handing a spoon and bowl to Max. He took a bite. "Thank you, dearest."

Burt set himself on the hay, while Deidre ate on the stump. "So, what are your plans?"

Max settled himself next to Burt on the hay pile. "We're heading to wherever there may be jobs. The general direction was London. But if there is any place nearby with some work?"

Burt grabbed the bottom of his chin. "Amersham is needing a lot of workers right now. Everything is building up. Good place to start. London can be so full of bustle. Hard to raise a family there. Two young people like you both need a good start."

Deidre eyed Max. "Anything you can tell us, we'll appreciate."

Max got up and gave her his empty bowl. She refilled it for Burt.

"Well, there is Old Man Vincent," he said taking the bowl from Max. "He's got a store in Amersham. And there is a factory there you could check into. They need a lot of good-handed folk there, even women." He eyed her up and down. "It's a shame to have you wearing men's clothes. I'm sure a pretty, young thing like you deserves a proper dress."

"I do what I must to survive."

"If you like, I can give you one of my wife's dresses to wear. I'd hate to see it not used."

"That's kind of you." She gave a smile toward Burt. "Where is it?"

"Back at my farm house. It's a walk out of the pasture and down the hill by the main road. You'll have to go that way on the way to Amersham. You might be able to hitch a ride to there as well."

Max stood. "We'd appreciate that. It's good to know that good people exist who will help others when they are down on their luck."

"It's no more than any good Christian would do."

"How about I take the bowls and wash them in the creek." Deidre took the dishes, and headed out the door.

"You've got quite a woman there."

Max watched Deidre walk through the door to the creek. "Yes. I know."

"Hold onto her."

"I intend to."

Burt looked lost in thought. "I can still remember the day I proposed. We were at church, and I had to get my nerve up to ask her. Finally, I got a moment alone with her, away from our families. We stole away to the river, and it was like all of nature held its breath. That's when I knew it was time."

"All of nature held its breath?" Max asked.

"Yes. It was strange. All sounds stopped. No birds sang. The burble of the creek stilled. I took it as a sign that moment froze for us. The universe waited for her answer."

"And she said yes."

"It was the worst and best moment of my life." He looked in the distance. "The horror of waiting to hear her answer turned into the sweet memorable yes from her lips." He looked over towards the opening to the shed. "I think that's what life is about. The ups and downs in one moment, make it worthwhile."

Deidre came back into the shed asking, "Where should I put these?" She had a cheerful tone as she held the stacked, clean bowls.

"Back in the storage bag should be fine." Deidre placed the bowls back into the sack.

Burt got up and headed to the opening. "Come on, you two. I'll show you a portrait of Peg when we get to the house."

Max looked at Deidre. She shrugged her shoulders, and the two of them followed Burt out of the shed.

Seventeen

The journey to Burt's house—the "walk out of the pasture and down the hill by the main road"—took the rest of the afternoon. They saw the house come into view as they came down out of the pasture to a gravel road. The farmhouse had a slanted thatch roof and was enclosed by a simple post fence with single boards. When they arrived, Max was walking next to Deidre. Burt had been talking about the last few years before his wife passed. It was clear he was enjoying their company, and sharing stories about his wife. All it took was a nod of encouragement to keep him talking while they figured out their next move.

"Nice church you have there. What's the name of the moor?" Max pointed. They were close enough to town to see the church steeple and a body of water in the distance. The moor rose as a fixture behind the town. The creek had emptied into a larger river as they moved away from it to Burt's house. Burt had mentioned it was the Misbourne.

Pushing his hat back so he could see the church, Burt looked to where Max was pointing. "Chesham Moor." Burt looked down. "Miss that church. There was the choir every Sunday. Peggy used to sing in it, but I hardly go now since she passed."

"Surely, they want you to still go to church." Deidre spoke supportively. "The pastor would want you to join them."

"Don't have the heart to go now. Just Rusty and me. And the sheep. I like to go check on the sheep. Gives me a routine."

Max gave Deidre a look. "It's near the center of town near the market, I believe. Amersham has always had a good market."

"Yes. You are right. This town is a good place to settle down. It had been a good home to Peg and me. It's not that far of a walk from here either."

"Then, that means the train station is nearby as well?"

Burt scratched his head. "I think about a twenty-minute walk from here. Why, you need to take the train? Amersham does have a station, but it will take money."

"We do have some money saved." Max answered. "For travel."

"Well then, if you're saving money for your future, I'd like to help. I'll have to give you the full tour of the town before you leave. Nice couple like you starting out on hard times could settle here though. Reminds me of Peg and I when we were young." He smiled and clapped his hands. "How 'bout you stay here. Rest up and maybe help me fix up some parts of my place."

"I'd be grateful for that. Maybe for a day then." Max held Deidre's hand.

She looked at Burt, smiling. He seemed so kind and lonely. "If you want, I'll clean some of your home. We don't want to be a burden, but help pay for our stay with some odd jobs."

"Of course. I could use some help. Things aren't the same as when Peg was here."

Burt led them up the path to the front door, surrounded by weed-infested roses. The paint of floral decorations around the windows was worn and peeling. Burt walked up the steps and pushed the door open. Brushing his feet off on the mat, he went inside. Max and Deidre followed.

The musty smell of dirt and old laundry filled the front room. There was a scrap rug on the dirt floor under a plain wooden table at its center. A cooking pot hung inside the fireplace, and a clock and a vase with dried flowers sat on the mantel above. A picture frame of a woman hung next to the clock.

Another picture of a young man and woman hung on the opposite wall. She was in a wedding dress, and he was dressed in a suit. Deidre pointed when she saw it. "Burt, that's you when you were younger. So, that means this is Peg."

"Yes. That was taken on our wedding day."

"You make a fine couple." Max stood in front of the picture. His eyes drifted to Deidre.

She looked back and nodded. "Let me see if there is some food for a dinner. Is there anything Mark can do for you Burt?"

Burt had been staring at the wedding photo. "Well, yes." He slapped his trousers, like he was looking for something. "Oh, here they are." He took out a pair of wire-rimmed glasses. "I will need some help stacking logs for the fire. My back isn't what it used to be."

"Sure thing." Max slapped his hands together. "Where's your wood pile?"

"Out back. I'll show you." Burt moved toward the back door, and Max followed. Looking back at Deidre, he whispered, "We're near my vehicle."

Her eyes grew wide. Max turned and left with Burt. He followed Burt to the woodpile and grabbed some logs with him. "Don't worry about this Burt. Go back inside and have Dee make you some tea. Take a load off. Relax. I'll bring in the wood."

"That's awfully kind of ya, Mark. Thank you."

He started to walk back to the house and turned. "Tell her you love her every day."

"What was that, Burt?" Max put the log he was holding down for a moment.

"Tell your wife every day that you love her. I don't think I did that enough. I don't want you making the same mistake. It's something you'll regret if you ever lose her."

Max looked down for a moment. Taking a deep breath, he shook his head. "You're right. It's a big mistake not to say it." He looked at Burt, and the men locked eyes. "You're a good soul, ole man."

Burt waggled his finger at him. "You're a young fool if you don't heed me."

"I'm young and stupid about many things. I agree. But I will tell her I love her, as soon as I get back in."

Burt came up and socked him in the arm. "That's better. You never know how much you love them until they're gone."

"That's too true."

Max watched Burt hobble back into his home. Stacking the logs on top of each other, he carried an armful back to the house, thinking about what he should say to Deidre. Burt couldn't know he'd already lost Deidre once. He wanted to really be her husband, not just play the role. He bit back a sigh.

He wanted to say it to her for real. I love you. Not while making love, but for what his heart felt all the time. The thing was, he wasn't truly sure if she felt the same. She hadn't really come out and said it, except when they were charging their bracelets. Would she say it on her own, not in the throes of passion?

He reached the door and nudged it open with his foot. "Wood's here."

"Good. Put it in a stack by the fire," Deidre's voice directed him. Max balanced the logs and made it to the spot she had pointed to. He placed the logs down, careful that they didn't roll out of their stack. Brushing his hands on his shirt, he said, "Is there tea for me?"

"Yes. I left a cup for you on the table." Deidre returned to cutting the vegetables she had stacked on the tabletop. Burt was sitting in a chair near the window, and there was a small wooden bench lined with blankets and pillows. Max headed over and took a seat next to Burt.

"At the end of the day, a man likes something a little stronger in his tea. Whiskey?"

Max nodded. Deidre stopped cutting for a moment. "You corrupting my husband, Burt?"

Burt got up and took a flask from the mantelpiece. "No. Just showing him good English hospitality." He went over and poured some into Max's and then his drink. Sitting back down, he clinked mugs with Max.

The fire lit the room as the sun began to set outside. Deidre tossed the last of the vegetables into the pot and set the stew over the fire to cook. "Burt, which candles do you prefer lit in the evening? It is going to be dark soon."

"In the rim of the windows there are some candles, and there is a lantern you can light on top of the mantel."

Deidre touched a small twig to the fire and went around the small home, lighting the candles and lantern. "This is such a nice little place, Burt."

"It is now, with company." He raised his mug to her.

"Very true." Max clinked against Burt's mug. "Good to know you, Burt."

After their drink, Burt said, "I was thinking of sleeping arrangements."

Deidre looked from the candle she was lighting. The candles gave her a surreal glow. "It would be nice to sleep in a proper home and not out on the land tonight."

"That's what I was thinking," Burt answered. "A couple should be in a proper bed. I can make a pallet in this room. You both can have the back room."

"But we don't want to put you out of your bed." Max put his hand to Burt's shoulder.

"No worries. You need to keep that wife warm. I gather you two could use a nice bed with what you've been through."

"Thank you." Deidre ran to Burt, wrapping her arms around his neck. "You are a dear."

He patted her back. "I had a daughter once. If she had survived, she'd be a lot like you, my dear." He drank the rest of the tea, and poured a little more whiskey in his cup.

The smell of stew filled the little house. Burt looked to Deidre. "Do you have plans for children soon?"

"When we get settled, I hope." She looked to Max. He had a dreamy cast to his face. They both knew that timeanauts didn't have children until after their mission period. In fact, children weren't a necessary thing for people in the future. They were a luxury created after a first career. Timeanauts waited until they were way past serving their missions at thirty-five or didn't have them at all. It wasn't a career that boded well for rearing a child. She never expected to have any.

Deidre looked at Max, and noticed her stomach felt unsettled. She wasn't sure if it was because of the water from yesterday or all that had happened. She stopped for a moment and took a sip from her tea. That seemed to settle it a little. But she still felt tired. She took a rest in the chair at the table, watching the men in conversation.

Time passed in polite conversation, during which Max passed looks back and forth with Deidre. It felt natural to pretend they were married. In fact, Deidre fell into the new role easily. It was a good cover for them both. She looked over to Max, his relaxed body leaning back against the pillows on the bench.

"Do you really think it would be that easy to get all the labor that factory needs?" Burt was asking Max. "Yes. In fact, I think that new factory is going to change the town," answered Max.

"The stew is almost ready." Deidre stood and started to swing the pot from the fire. She had a bowl that she spooned into, and handed it off to Max. Then, the next she filled and handed to Burt. She took her bowl last. Her stomach gurgled when she smelled the food. It was nauseating, and she had to take a drink of tea to settle her stomach again. She did not want to tell Max. He'd tease her, boasting that he had been right about the water.

In a moment, the sick feeling passed, and her stomach began to growl with hunger. Strange. Her body seemed to be acting funny the last few days. It must be the shock.

There was a peaceful silence while everyone ate. It was broken by Burt's comment. "Dee, this stew is wonderful. It's as good as Peg's."

She nodded to him. "Thank you."

"It's why I married her. She's such a good cook." Max winked at Deidre. He knew what courses timeanauts took to train for living in the past.

She winked back. Cooking was one of the major classes of training. It was a lost art and more of a hobby in her time now. She nodded and smiled. It was pleasant for her to play the demure country wife. She hadn't expected to be playing a role like this. It was very satisfying to use some of the skills she'd learned.

It was a confirmation that her cooking was good too, and it settled her nerves. She didn't want to blow this new cover. They were Time Rogues now. She wasn't sure what would happen. It seemed keeping to her new role was their best option, but she missed being a poet already. She always felt drawn to art, but this simple life would do for now.

The men continued their conversation about the new factory while Deidre washed the bowls and spoons in the washbasin. She towel-dried them while the men had another drink. She could almost pretend she belonged in this time.

Burt waved his hands around to emphasize his point. "But, Max, you've got to see how this would be the wrong thing for the town. It's going to change everything."

"That's my point. It's progress. This is a new century. Manufacturing is key. It is our future."

Deidre piped in. She looked at Max while wiping her hands on the apron. "That's right." She walked over and placed her hand on his shoulder. "It could be our future."

Both men stopped to turn and look at her. Burt asked, "What do you mean, my dear?"

She looked at Max. "I mean, it could be our future." She captured his eyes with her words. "We could stay here, maybe pay rent, and help out Burt. When the factory opens, we could get jobs there."

Burt answered, "It will be a few more months before it opens."

"We can wait. Can't we?" She tried to hide the longing in her voice. He had to see it wasn't an act.

"We'll have to discuss it." Max's voice had gotten very low.

Burt looked at them both. "I think it's a great idea. You both could help me out, and when you're able, pay rent from your salaries. I do need help around here."

"Please, Max." She grabbed his shoulder tighter. "We can stay for a little while, can't we?"

"For now, we must keep our visit short. A day at most. The market, Burt? We're near Amersham, correct?"

"Yes. Tomorrow is market day," Burt replied. "I can take you there, if you want."

"Yes. That would help, Burt. We'll need to see what we can pick up before we meet up with a colleague of mine." Max looked at Deidre. "He had a lead on a job. James is his name."

Deidre said. "Yes. You agreed to meet him and follow up on that lead."

"Well, I can take you both tomorrow then." The fire had died down, and Burt started to yawn. "I don't know about you, but I'm feeling quite tired. I usually turn in just a little after the sun goes down."

As if his yawn was a signal, Deidre yawned too. "I don't think I've been sleeping well lately. But turning in early sounds wonderful. I think this country air and a comfortable bed are just what I need."

"Fine, then," Burt said. "In fact, if you help a bit, we can make a pallet for me by the fire, and the room is all yours."

They helped him get the front room all settled with his sleeping pallet, took a candle in with them, and closed the door. Finally, they were alone. It didn't take long for them to hear Burt's snores coming from the front room.

"What do you think?" Deidre's eyes sparked with excitement while she held the candle.

"We can stay maybe a few days, tops, under the pretense of helping him. This is a good cover to hide for just a little while. We can get ready to jump. I might be able to hide my time vehicle closer."

Her pout spoke about what she was thinking. He pulled her closer. "You wanted to stay longer?"

"It would be so nice to not worry about research or jumping for a while."

His eyebrow went up. "Our departure has nothing to do with continuing your research. You haven't forgotten about the agents chasing us, correct? Not to mention the local law enforcement that thinks we're swindlers."

She looked at him, her smile waning. Her shoulders sank. "I was so hoping for a little more time playing husband and wife."

She placed the candle down on the small table by the bed. She turned and wrapped her arms around his neck. "I'm having fun being domestic. I haven't had to play a role like this in a while. Not since…" She bit her lip.

He wrapped his arms around her waist. "Not since James."

"No. I've been solo since my last jump. That was months ago now." She looked down. Some of her hair fell in her face.

He pulled it back and tucked it behind her ear. "This isn't hard for you is it?"

"No. I'm enjoying being your wife." She leaned closer nuzzling against his chest. "It's nice to pretend."

He leaned her back on the bed. "I'd gladly make you my wife for real."

She put her hand on his chest to stop him. "Wait. Is that a proposal?"

He leaned over her, his cheek caressing against hers. He whispered, "It can be. If you want it to."

She pressed her cheek against his. "It would be kind of hard to get married when we already are."

"We can make it official when we get back to our time."

She pulled away and looked deep into his eyes. "You're serious."

"More than I've ever been." Max held his breath.

Deidre closed her eyes. "I don't know what to say."

"Say yes."

"I don't know if I can. I don't think I could take this kind of hurt again. I want to be with you." She nuzzled against his neck. "What we do is dangerous. We've got people after us. We don't even know if we can go back to our time."

"Not too long ago, you wanted to be my wife."

"I want to be something of yours. But committing to long-term anything is too irrational. Nothing we have could be long term."

He put his hand on her cheek. "You don't mean that."

"I don't mean between us. I mean with anybody. From mission to mission, we don't know what could happen. We have to be so careful to not change the past. But then, now we don't even know if we can go back to our time." She wrapped her arm around him. They moved closer, feeling the warmth of each other. "It's not necessarily marrying you. It's marrying anybody. I don't think I can."

He looked into her eyes. "Then, I'll take what I can have. I can have you. Here. In the now." Their limbs mingled. "I want to show you how I love you."

She caressed his jaw, running her fingers down the stubble on his neck. She had come to know that face in the short time they'd had together, comfortable with their intimacy. But this time felt different. A tingling shot through her arm. Her body felt like it was on a greater vibration, attuning to Max. He kissed her, pulling her lip, mingling their tongues in a dance she so understood. She was moving in rhythm to his attentions, like they were a well-oiled machine.

He unbuttoned the front of her simple cotton dress, and she lifted her breasts to greet his caress. And then she fell…right down the rabbit hole she was dreading. She didn't want to love. She closed her eyes. But she felt herself longing for his touch. She opened her eyes, and took a breath to calm her fear.

Max stopped. "What is it?"

"I'm afraid."

He pulled her closer. "Of what?"

"Of loving you."

"Love is the greatest thing. It is the only thing that can stop fear."

She kissed his neck. "I don't want to lose you, Max. Ever. But what lies ahead of us, we have no idea."

"Then all we can promise each other is now. And I'm here now. We're loving each other now."

She closed her eyes again. "So we promise to love each other… for now?"

"Yes. It is the best way to love."

Their lips melted into each other. Max pulled Deidre to sit up, moving her dress down and off her body while Deidre undid Max's shirt buttons. Their kiss took on a life of its own, as their bodies rocked in time with the removal of their clothes. Their lips fought to be together in the frenzy of making the other naked.

Deidre felt the wetness grow between her legs just thinking about an intimate connection. Max lay across her, moving his body up and down, kissing her in the places he knew she liked best. Her body began to tremble with each new kiss. Between her breasts, down her stomach, Max's lips tickled her flesh, sending electrical sparks through Deidre. Her mind was overwhelmed by the feeling he was building in her.

"Deidre."

"Yes."

"Love me in the now."

"I do. I love you. Now."

Max's lips met hers, and she moved her arms around him. Their bodies pulsed in a rhythm perfectly aligned. Max pressed against Deidre's breasts with his chest. He looked into her eyes. "I love you now and forever." He slipped his hand between her thighs, pressing inward with his thumb, feeling the wetness of her flowering center. "I'll take all your love and hold it in my heart forever." He pulled his hand away, replacing it with his manhood as he eased himself into her wet opening. She welcomed him by pushing against him, opening her legs wider. "Whether we end together or not, I love you now."

Deidre rolled her eyes back, raising her hips to drive him into her very being. He moved back and forth building the feelings in both of them. The hiss of passion fell out of Deidre as his final thrust pushed her over the edge. Her body felt like it scattered apart, leaving her mind blank and completely lost to Max.

When she came back to herself, Max lay next to her, twirling her hair. "My love. Deidre. Are you all right?"

"I've never felt that before."

"Your orgasm?"

"No. I've felt that before, but never that intense."

She turned toward Max, propping herself up on her elbow. Her breasts just barely pressed against his arm. "I lost myself to you, Max."

"I lost myself too."

She looked into his eyes. "Is that love?"

He kissed her, pulling her closer to him. "Yes. You love me now?"

"Yes." She lifted her free hand and reached around to rub his neck. "I never thought I'd feel like this again. But somehow it's different."

"How so?"

"It's stronger."

He kissed her again, pushing her deep in the hay mattress. Their legs tangled together. Arms wrapped around each other, Max fell asleep on Deidre's shoulder. Her heart filled in a new way. She closed her eyes with thoughts of what it might be like to be Max's wife, not just now, but in the future.

Eighteen

They went to the market in Amersham the next day. With their bracelets charged, they knew they could make a jump soon. If they could make a jump to 1928, they would already be at the rendezvous location to meet up with James. They kept their eyes out for the Time Council operatives. It would be the only wrench in their plan if agents found them now.

It was a nice, crisp summer morning that the three found themselves walking into town. The market was set up on Tuesdays, and the town was bustling with activity for market day. They had agreed to help Burt shop for his weekly supplies before they met up with their friend, James. Deidre didn't have the heart to tell Burt they wouldn't return to the farm with him.

They had been walking down the sidewalk towards the market hall. That's when Deidre spotted someone unusual. A man that seemed to be dressed a little more well-to-do than the locals. He kept looking in their direction, trying to stay hidden behind a newspaper he read. Leaning against the wall of the local pub across the street, he would look over the paper to where they were standing.

Deidre nudged Max. "That man over by the pub. He is staring at us quite a lot."

"Really?" Max didn't move his head. "What makes you think so?"

"He reminds me of the way you used to watch me. However, he is much more creepy."

He reached for her hand. "Let's see if he follows. If we walk around the market hall, it will be hard to see what we're doing." He turned to Burt. "Maybe if we try the other side of the market, we'll find better prices."

"Not usually. I've known most of these people for years. This is the best spot for fresh potatoes."

Deidre piped up. "I do want to see if there are any apples better than these. Maybe green apples for a pie."

Burt's face lit up. "You only had to say the word 'pie.' I'll show you the best apples in all of Amersham."

They followed Burt's lead. Deidre chanced looking back for a moment to see if the man was following. He folded his paper under his arm and began to walk a distance behind them. She squeezed Max's hand. "He's following."

"Damn." Max swore under his breath. "I was afraid they might find us."

"What do we do?"

"We may have to jump ahead after all."

"When?"

He grabbed her hand. "Now."

She didn't miss a beat in her step, but swallowed. "What about Burt?"

"He'll be fine." He led Deidre by the hand, watching as Burt made his way through the market stalls.

"Isn't the time vehicle near here?" asked Deidre.

"Yes. On the other side of town by the river. I've had it moving to this position since this morning." He stopped for a moment, swiped and tapped his bracelet. "It will meet us along the river's edge. You ready for this?"

"Do I have a choice?"

"Not if you want to jump together. We'll not want to be caught. James is counting on me to save you."

"I'm sure he'll be thankful you did." She bit her lip. She didn't want to think about meeting James after all this time. What do you say to a dead lover when you love another? She couldn't sort it in her mind.

The best she could do was get out of this time with Max. They'd have the time-jump in 1928 to sort out everything. Burt would have to always wonder what happened to them. There was no time for a good-bye.

"I'm going to miss Burt." She watched his waddling form disappear into the crowd. His feet scraped against the dirt, kicking up a little cloud behind him.

Max turned to watch Burt leaving. "I will too."

"Don't make a move." Deidre felt a something hard press into her back. A man's voice whispered in her ear. "Don't move, Deidre. You were supposed to be dead, anyway. The timeline would have been fixed that way." She heard a shuffle next to her. "Don't you move either, Max. It would be easier if I killed her right now."

"What are you going to do?" Max's voice was cautious and controlled.

"What I was sent here to do. Fix the timeline." The man moved her hair away from her neck. "That means if I have to kill you, I will, dear girl."

Deidre swallowed. "You can't do that here. Any time period seems to react badly to murder in public."

"Then we'll go somewhere that isn't public." He pressed what she was sure was a gun into her back, and pushed her from behind. "Move forward slowly. If you do anything, Max, she's dead."

"I didn't expect an agent to find us so easily." Deidre looked over to Max to see him looking around.

"Dismantling the digital tracker in the vehicle only delayed me." The man huffed. "Your control bracelets are traceable. But that does take time. Max reactivated his. Sad. Too bad you didn't think to stay in this time. It would have been harder to track you."

Deidre looked to Max. His face held tension. His eyes continued to look around. She kept looking to see what she could do. People still walked around them in the market. She was safe as long as they stayed there. If the agent could find a location where they'd be alone, she was dead. "You know, there has got to be a way the Time Council can fix the timeline without me dead."

"It's not because of you. It's the baby."

"What baby?"

"The one you have. And that changes everything."

She kept talking. Maybe she could get him to see reason. "Well, I have no baby now. And pregnancy isn't possible with my NaNoBots and implant." She tried to turn and face the agent, but he shoved her again. "Unless something deactivated them."

"Stop talking and don't try turning around. It's all decided. You have to die. Going rogue really wasn't a solution."

Deidre started, "But Max?"

"He'll be prosecuted. But leaving you in this time or any time is too dangerous. Now, move across the street. I want to head down to the river where there are fewer people." Again, the man reminded her of the gun at her back, forcing her to cross the street. She started across, with Max skirting next to her. She grabbed Max's hand.

The agent pushed them apart. "Let him go. I don't want any contact between you."

"You'll execute me without any other reason. At least the condemned in this time might get a cigarette."

Their feet scraped along the dust. She coughed slightly. The man pushed her harder. "Keep going. I don't want stalling."

"If you think I'm going to just let you kill me," she started.

The man cut her off. "No. I didn't think that. That's why I've brought some help," he said, "Keep going. We're almost there."

She heard a crack behind her. Max spun and hit the man with the gun. Burt was behind her, hitting the other man. She knew that it was time to do something, but was frozen to the spot. Max was struggling with the gun, battling the man for control. He shouted, "Run, Deidre."

The gun fired, and she looked back to see Max struggling with the agent. The other man started running toward Burt as she heard another shot go off. She saw Max slump down. She screamed. That's when the agent turned and started firing at her. She ran, zigzagging to be a difficult target, down to the river where Max had said the time vehicle was waiting. As she ran along the river's edge, she heard shouting and people moving that direction to see what was going on.

It took all of her resolve to keep moving. It was like what had happened with James. A sudden ambush. Too many people kept trying to kill her, and the men she loved saved her.

She ran and ran. She felt the beat of her feet hitting the dirt of the towpath The thumps of her shoes against the hard dirt of the river's edge were her only indication of her progress. She kept moving forward until she could see the bridge that would take her over to the side with the time vehicle.

When she got to the bridge, she looked back. No one was following. She must have lost them. She leaned on the bridge railing for support. Her breath came in ragged gulps until her body finally caught up. She looked up and saw some people strolling about, having no awareness of what had happened closer to town. She wasn't sure if Max was okay. But she couldn't risk going back, for fear there were more agents.

Once she got her breath back, she headed over the bridge, but kept looking around for signs of someone following. She mulled over what the agent had said. She was already dead. Max, if he survived, would be imprisoned for a while. But he wouldn't be killed. There must be an order out to kill her at all costs. But why? She had thought that the only thing that changed the time-line was keeping Henri from going to war. But what was this talk of a baby?

Maybe Max hadn't told her everything. The thought shot through her like a lightning bolt. She had to have done something more that made the Time Council want her killed on sight instead of just apprehended. She looked over toward the other side of the bridge. Then, she let her eyes sweep around to see if anyone was noticing her. She had to be careful. Max was right about one thing. She needed to get away and solve this.

She started across the bridge, giving a quick look behind, and that's when she saw him. Another man, dressed in very well-to-do clothes. She knew an agent always chose the best clothes of the period. You could fit in a lot of places to research that way. He spotted her and started to walk faster toward where she was on the bridge.

She picked up her pace, noticing that the people were growing fewer in number. She built up her speed. If she could make it to the time vehicle, she would be safe. She broke into a brisk walk, and he picked up speed behind her. She focused on making it to the vehicle, looking for a car parked along the canal path. She could hear his footfalls catching up. She broke into a run.

All her concentration turned to running. She had to make it to the vehicle. No matter what happened, she knew she'd be dead if she were caught now. The farm dress skirts flew to the sides as she made it across the bridge. Sprinting across the field, she could hear her pursuer. Damn. She couldn't end it this way. She hit the button on the bracelet to signal an emergency and guide her to the nearest time vehicle. She waved her hand in front of her, and felt the vibration of which direction to run. She headed that way, finding the vehicle behind some bushes where Max must have hidden it. Placing her palm on the window, the keypad recognized her from Max's programming. She flung the door open and climbed in.

As she tried to close the door, she was stopped by someone pulling from the other side. She tugged, and got it to shut. A bullet rang out and ricocheted off the vehicle. The auto shield turned on, changing the door to its true form, which had no handle, and sealed her in. She could hear the bullets bouncing off the outside.

She unclicked her crystal from her bracelet, and inserted it into the energy slot. The vehicle powered up. She started shouting. "Program to jump to 1928. Move to the road in the form of a 1914 Napier T78 coupe." She couldn't think of any other form to take but that of her car from the trip to this time. She felt the hard form reshape into a seat and cushions. She looked at the newly formed back window and saw men running after her. "Faster speed to outdistance the men chasing us."

The computer voice answered her. "Exact speed needed."

"Increase to thirty-five kilometers per hour."

The time vehicle moved through the grassy field, outdistancing the running men. She kept looking back to make sure they were still behind her. "Head to the London Road so we can make a jump to the programmed year."

"Roger, Timeanaut Deidre."

She eased back against the cushioned seat. She pursed her lips, wondering if she could double back and find Max. "Give location of Timeanaut Max. Is he alive?"

The computer voice ticked back. "He is alive, but wounded. He is currently with Agents Frank, Damian, Clark, and Buckley. He is currently resisting arrest."

"Damn it." The vehicle continued to roll across the field. She snapped her fingers. "What does the timeline say right now? What happens to him?"

"Agent Max is currently being escorted to another time. Agents Johnson and Harris are still in pursuit of rogue Agent Deidre."

"What is the status of Agent Deidre?"

"Rogue Agent."

"Can I still jump?"

"No readjustments have been programmed into this vehicle. No updates have been received. All communications have been adjusted to receive only updates, but no cancellations from Time Council Command."

Deidre shook her head. Tears started to form in her eyes. She could jump and leave Max behind, and try to find James. Or she could try to figure out a way to save Max before she jumped. Behind her, she noticed a car following. It was similar to hers, and had to be another agent's time vehicle. It seemed all but impossible to save Max. Not with other agents right behind her, and with him already in custody. She had to think.

"What is the year they are scheduled to take him to?"

"The first jump is scheduled in two days for the year 1928."

"Brilliant. If I jump now, I could intercept." She looked ahead at the road. Behind her, she could still see the other time vehicle closing in. "Damn. They'll follow for sure. Especially if I go to the same year. I'll just have to go earlier, and hide for a while until they arrive."

The car behind sped up and rammed the back of her. She was done with thinking. She had to act. "Reprogram the jump to 1927."

"Acknowledged." The computer voice sounded comforting. It was something she was familiar with.

She looked behind her one more time, and saw the car coming at her for another ram. Looking ahead she gave the order. "Make jump time in one minute." A countdown started on the panel. The time vehicle beeped three times. She looked behind, noticing the car was speeding up again. "Increase speed to fifty kilometers an hour. We need to outrun the car behind us."

"Acknowledged." The vehicle sped up, and the other vehicle matched her speed. They rammed her again, this time knocking her so hard she lifted off the cushion. "Jump in thirty seconds." The car behind rammed again, and her teeth cracked against each other with the impact. "Jump in ten seconds. Nine. Eight." She saw the vehicle from behind try to move up alongside to knock her off the road. It was a race. If they really wanted her to go that way, she could. They wouldn't expect it. "Steer off the road into that field."

"Acknowledged. Four. Three." The other vehicle veered off to follow. "Two. One."

Nausea and black out. She was falling and then she felt the stillness of the jump. She must have passed out, and woke to see that it was a clear day outside. Her vehicle was on the side of the dirt road. The fields looked the same, but the other agent's vehicle was not alongside hers.

"Choosing a vehicle transformation."

An image of a Rolls Royce 1926 Phantom appeared on the console screen. "Formation is complete." The voice was very similar to Max's intonation but with a computer monotone. She wondered if it had picked it up from him. Funny, how she didn't notice it when she was first being chased. It made her miss him more. "New transformation to begin in five, four, three, two, one." The vibration in the walls told her the transformation was in progress. The seats shifted under her and took on a new design.

"Vehicle transformation complete. Awaiting timeanaut instructions."

What was in England 1927? She reviewed the panel to see what was in the area. She was still near Amersham. She could head back to Hampstead. She could stay at the cute inn that the elderly woman ran, if she were still alive. Of course, it was over a decade later. It could have new owners. But if she could find a way to just wait for the jump Max would make in a year, maybe she could save him somehow. After all, she had a year to plan.

Then she remembered what the agent had said. She looked at her bracelet and removed a second crystal. The bracelet beeped once. She opened a compartment inside the vehicle and stashed the crystal and bracelet inside. "They won't be able to find me now. I won't be able to jump for a while, but I'll definitely be safe from discovery until Max arrives." Smiling, she set the coordinates to travel back into Amersham.

She drove into the town and parked the car, then got out to look around. She walked down the cobblestone streets, and passed where she'd shopped at the market with Max and Burt. Thinking back to what was her yesterday made Deidre realize that the town had built up a lot. It was then that she noticed a man coming toward her. A man whose face she'd never forget. She couldn't mistake his blue eyes and curly blond hair, no matter what suit in any time he wore. It was James.

Nineteen

Deidre walked down Amersham's main street, nodding to the people she had met over the last year. She kept her hands on the handle of the pram, careful not to wake the little infant inside. One more day. Tomorrow would mark exactly one year since she'd jumped, leaving Max in 1914. Tomorrow, Max should jump to her time. Of course, he would most likely have the two agents with him, but she had a lot of ideas in full play. He wouldn't expect this. She looked down at the baby sound asleep, and stopped to rock him gently. She smiled. He wouldn't expect the plan she had in mind.

"Good morning, Mrs. Henderson." A lady said cheerfully as she passed.

"Good morning, Mrs. Carpenter." Deidre smiled and waved. She and James had assumed the names Nellie and John Henderson. Over the last year, she'd gotten to know many of the local people while renting a little cottage near the city center. It was a nice walk there and back for her supplies. She had enjoyed the pretense of living as a newlywed, trying to write her first poetry collection. She had actually done a good amount of writing, and finished not one, but two collections.

She was disappointed to think that nothing was to become of them. But at the very least, she was taking them with her to see if something could happen with them later. She had never taken anything with her before when jumping from one period to another, but she had stowed them in the time vehicle just in case. It was, after all, a year's worth of work. Maybe she could sell them in another time period. As most poets and writers do, she had simply written them for herself. But she couldn't part with them. It was something that was a part of her now. That much, she could take with her from doing research.

The clicking of her heels on the paved stones gave a rhythm to her thoughts. The relaxed atmosphere of the last year had maybe put her too much at ease. Would she be ready for the agents when they arrived? She wasn't sure. Instincts were sure to kick in.

She adjusted her hat, a nice round felt design with a band around its center, without missing her step. She made the perfect picture of a new mother. Her simple wool skirt and linen blouse made her feel more like a teacher, but the outfit was more appropriate for her new station in this life. She didn't care for the flamboyant colors or dresses she had loved to wear on other missions. She wanted not to be noticed, at least for now. Not since she had come here had she realized that so much could change in a year.

Her thoughts drifted back to Max. She tried to concentrate as she continued walking. She could still remember his lips on hers. The way his hands felt when he caressed her. It hadn't been this bad when she'd lost James. She still felt she would always be close to James, but the longing for Max was different.

She heard footsteps behind her. She tried to not turn. He was supposed to meet her at the pub, but maybe he had something else in mind. She felt an arm come up behind her, wrapping around her waist. She stopped and received a gentle kiss to her cheek.

"How are you doing, sweetheart?" The man was wearing a double-breasted dark suit. It was so popular in this time. It looked good on him.

She smiled, eyeing him up and down. "Wonderful." She didn't hide her sarcasm. "I'm trying not to think about tomorrow." She looked at him, watching his hair flop down into his blue eyes. She had loved his look when he stared at her like that. Her feelings were in such upheaval. James was with her again, but all she could think about was Max.

It hadn't taken long for James to explain why he had been there waiting for her when she jumped. He had arrived early, knowing she would jump because of the fight. He was privy to the new timeline. The agents weren't. The Time Rogues had blocked their updates. Now, they were just a day away from Max's fateful jump. Everything that they had planned for a year would happen tomorrow.

"Well, try to be careful until it's time. We don't want to alert the agents that we're here." He got closer and moved some of her hair behind her ear. "You're thinking about him, aren't you?"

"I'm hoping he's okay. That's all."

"We've been through so much already together, babe. Saving Max is the least we can do for him. After all, he saved you for me." He leaned in to kiss her, and she looked away. "What is it?"

"It's just that now that he is almost here, I'm not sure what I want."

He lifted her chin. "You want to help Max, right?"

"Yes."

"Then, I promised I'd meet him here, and we'd save him. You just happened to get here first, with the ultimate surprise. He didn't know about what I'd put on the locket."

"No." She looked at his eyes. "I didn't expect the little surprise to come out of what you put on the locket either.." She looked down at the baby.

He held her hands, drawning her eyes from the baby back to him. She licked her lips before speaking. "I didn't expect him." She pursed her lips and took a deep breath. "I don't know if I can let him go."

"It's for the best that we give him up for now. He is the new Rogue Leader if we do. If we leave him here, he'll be raised by the Rogue Resistance. He'll grow up. We'll see him in the next jump." He kissed her fingertips. Then, held her hands. "We can teach him what he needs to know then."

He looked up. "The Time Council is losing its grip on the tyranny of controlling time travel. They've had the power for too long. He is the new hope. You have brought us that." He whispered into her ear. "What does it feel like to be the mother of the Resistance?"

"It's just so hard to comprehend that I got mixed up in it." She couldn't look him in the eye.

"You didn't. I did. And it's all been to save you." He squeezed her hands.

She shook her head. "That's the part that is hard for me to accept."

"Max knew the risks when he went back to save you." He slipped his hand behind her back. "Let's follow our normal routine. We're going for our family stroll. Tomorrow will be market day, the date Max will jump to this time. We'll save him." He squeezed her hand. "Don't worry."

"You've said that before. Last time, you died, James."

"But this time, I won't." He brought up her hand and kissed it again. "I promise."

They walked a little longer. Deidre got lost in her thoughts for Max. His baby was in the stroller, the reason the agents had been after them both. Max still had no idea James had sent the locket to counteract their NaNoBots with nanoparticles, resulting in her pregnancy and the birth of their son. She was scared of what would happen tomorrow. Last time she'd made a jump with him, James hadn't made it. The thought of keeping balance echoed through her mind. Her son whimpered in his sleep, and she stopped a moment to put the blanket over him more, tucking him in.

James stopped to put his arm on her back, leaning next to her. "They'll come to take him tomorrow. You know it's for the best."

"Yes. I know." Deidre gently touched her baby's face. "If they knew I was his mother, he'd be hunted. We need to keep him a secret." She straightened his blanket. "He needs to grow up. If I'm near him, I'll put him in danger."

"The Resistance will keep him safe. When we meet him after the next jump, he'll be almost a man."

She straightened, keeping her head down, holding back the tears. "I don't know if I can do it, James."

He pulled her closer and stroked her hair. "You know it is the best thing for him. It's the best thing for us."

He brushed her lips with his. She closed her eyes. Emotions welled in her. "I'll miss him growing up."

"He'll grow up in the blink of an eye." He tilted her head up with his finger so she'd open her eyes. "Now, let's go spend one last night together, just like it was a normal night. It is the one thing we can do together, savor this moment as a family."

He wrapped his arms around her. This moment would be perfect, except she couldn't stop thinking about Max. James was so different now, and with the baby, her mind was so out of sorts. Her heart was in her throat, wondering what would happen tomorrow. Could they save Max? Would something happen to any of them?

She began to feel the pain of loss starting again, and James held her closer. "I'm sorry to put you through so much, Deidre. But tomorrow will be a new beginning."

She wiped a tear from her face. "You're right. Tonight we will be together. As a family." She turned to push the pram to the cottage steps. James grabbed the front, helping to lift it to the porch and to the top of the steps. Deidre reached in for her son, then gently pulled him to her chest, softly rubbing his back.

Soon, she wouldn't feel his soft skin. His mouth made a burble sound, and she adjusted him as he settled back into sleep. James put his arm around Deidre, and they walked into the house, leaving the pram facing the street. All looked like a normal early twentieth-century family settling in for the night. Deidre knew they were anything but that.

She arrived at the center of town where the Old Market Hall stood. The red-bricked market building was almost three hundred years old. It had changed some, with more pavement installed, cobbles redone, but the clock tower still overlooked the village from its rooftop on the edge of the market square. It would be near here that the fight happened fourteen years ago. Most likely if they jumped, they would come here.

She tried not to think of what had happened that morning. She knew her baby was safe in another's care. She tried not to think about anything but saving Max. She would be near tears if she did.

Now, she had to force herself through the second half of the plan. To coordinate with James. He was hidden on another part of the street. They had come up with a secret ambush as their best option.

Deidre would hide in a small recess between two buildings. It held a door and a small walkway. It couldn't rightly be called an alley. It was more a space between the two old buildings leading to the door to another building behind. The building before the other stuck out, and it was hard to tell if there was an opening. It was the perfect place to hide in wait, and pull someone away without being noticed…or followed. The plan was for James to bump into one of the agents. Then Deidre could pull Max away from them while they were distracted, and they wouldn't see where she took him. If it went well. She hoped it would.

The problem was they didn't know how the agents would be arranged walking down the street. They would have to wait and see. She hoped they made an appearance soon. She couldn't wait to see Max. They had parked the time vehicle across the bridge in a makeshift parking lot used on market day. It would be easy access for them to get away. She was still hoping his bracelet would be fully charged. It was part of her plan.

She wore fake glasses, as well as a hat, to disguise her true identity. Deidre watched the shoppers going by as she walked around the stalls in market hall. They were all set up with tables displaying fruits and vegetables or other wares on upturned wooden boxes. She smiled when she looked at some apples. She was still sad she never got a chance to make Burt his pie.

She walked by some tables displaying flowers creating the scent of spring in the air. She had bought a few items to fit into the scene. She moved around, going in and around the brick archways looking like a regular shopper, until she got in position. She could see James standing across the street reading a newspaper. He nodded over the top signaling they were coming.

Then, she saw him. The first agent. The one who had been chasing her down by the bridge. He was walking with the man that had held a gun to her back. Luckily, she was prepared for that too. She patted the gun in her purse. Just in case. She was hoping to outsmart them with her plan, and not need it. But having a gun now was going to be necessary as a Rogue. She didn't want to be caught again with one in her back and not have recourse. The thing she had been waiting for was not there. Max was not there.

She looked to see if there was anyone else behind them while keeping an eye on the two men. She kept looking back and forth, between the two men and where they might be going. James signaled across the street to follow them. She sped up to fall in behind. Neither looked back. She smiled. She could see the backs of their heads, and they were still wearing their clothes from 1914. They must have just arrived.

She assumed they must have done something with Max. Then, her thoughts led her to the alternative. They had killed him. But she wouldn't let her brain focus on that. If she could follow and find out what they did with him, it would give her an idea of what to do. James kept pace with her across the street.

She watched the men cross the road and weave between some cars. She followed, looking like she was just one of the many busy shoppers on market day. Finally, they ducked off into an alley and turned into the doorway of a local pub.

It was one of the places where she liked to come and write in the middle of the day. She smiled. They were in her territory now. She walked into the pub, and headed to the bar. She scanned the room quickly and spotted them in a far corner, ordering food.

"Nellie, you've come in for your normal fare today?"

"Yes, Ted," she answered. "I'll take a poor man's lunch and some cider. Got more to write later today."

"How's the baby? John taking care of him today?"

She didn't look in his eyes. If she did, she'd well up. "Actually, I left him with Mrs. Miller today. John is joining me for lunch."

"He's a cute little tyke." He went back to rubbing a glass dry as she looked over the room, trying not to look at the agents directly. Ted came back and handed her a pint of cider. She sipped it standing by the bar, watching the men from the corner of her eye. If she got closer, she might be able to hear what they were saying, but she didn't want to get too close or they might recognize her.

"Hey, Ted, I'll be over there. Is the morning paper in yet?"

"Yes. There are some pub copies over there in the corner."

She made her way over to the area where newspapers were left and exchanged by patrons. Taking a copy, she returned to the bar, but this time took a seat down near the men, positioning herself with her back to them. The door opened, and James came into the pub.

He walked over and sat next to her, giving her a kiss on the cheek. "Hi, honey. Getting some lunch?"

She nodded leaning closer to him and whispered, "I'm watching the agents over there."

He whispered back. "We can move to the booth next to them."

She nodded, picked up her cider and newspaper, and they moved to slide into the booth next to the agents. She took the side that put her back to the agents.

Ted walked over to the men. "What can I get you, gentlemen?"

"Your special of the day for three. Can you wrap one up for us to take with us?"

"Of course. You need one for an extra mate?"

The agent that had pointed the gun at her answered, "You can say that. He is like a mate."

They waited for Ted to leave. Deidre hid behind her paper. She heard one of the men speak. "You sure you tied him up tight enough?"

"He can't get out of my knots. Rope from 1914 is not as good as our synth, but it will hold 'im."

"Incarceration is too good for him. If I had my choice, I'd shoot him now. Less trouble than hauling him all the way back for the Council." Deidre held her breath.

"Yeah. But you missed the girl. Bringing one in is better than none."

They stopped talking for a while. Deidre pretended to read her paper, trying to keep the paper from shaking in her hands.

Ted startled her by bringing her food. "Here you go, Nellie. Glad to hear you're almost done with your manuscript." Turning to James, he smiled and said, "Nice to see you. Nellie says Mrs. Miller is watching over the little one today."

James nodded. "Yes, she's a blessing. The baby loves her."

"Good for you two. It's good for a young couple to get some quality time away from the baby. Now what can I get for you?"

James grabbed Deidre's hand, squeezing it. Deidre felt the tears held back by his touch. "Just the soup of the day. Eating light today, and a stout."

"I'll bring them right out. You both enjoy your time together."

Deidre answered, "I think we will. We need it. Thanks, Ted." She looked down at her food and dug into it to look like she was hungry. She hoped her hat hid her face enough while she ate. She heard the other man start again. "Hopefully Johnson and Harris catch up with Deidre. She's going to be the key to the whole downfall of the Council unless she's caught in time."

"You're telling me. If only Max had just let her die. Things would be so much easier. If her baby is born, the whole course of the Council will be changed."

Deidre let out a gasp. The men looked up, and she quickly picked up the paper and hid her face. She started eating again to cover her shock. Just then, Ted brought the men their food, along with the extra one—clearly for Max, wherever he was.

Ted then set down James's soup. "Another pint, Nellie?"

"Sure. I need some cider to relax." She grabbed James's hand again. "Not much time to relax lately. This pint is nice."

"Not to mention sleep." Ted winked at the both of them and went to pull her another pint. The men got up to leave. She watched them head to the door.

Damn. She didn't want to lose them. James threw a pound note on the table to cover the bill and headed for the door. Deidre caught up to Ted at the bar. "As a matter of fact, Ted, I think I'll pass on the last one. The cider is going straight to my head today."

He stopped in mid pull. Dumping the contents into a spittoon, he said, "Sure, if you say so." As she turned to go, he tapped the bar. "Good luck."

"Thank you." She followed James out the door and looked around to see which way the men had gone. The agents had headed back down the street to the market square.

James and Deidre fell in behind them. They had the advantage of being more familiar with the streets of the town in this time. She avoided the pothole as they crossed into the square, and weaved between the stalls so as to not draw their attention. They had to be heading back to the time vehicle and Max. They wouldn't be able to do a full jump until they charged their bracelets and rested from the previous jump. They were probably going to have to go into London to a brothel to do that. At least, if one guarded Max, that would give James and her an advantage. But first, the agents had to lead them to the time vehicle.

They passed through the market and headed for the bridge. She smiled. The agents continued over the bridge and down along the river's edge. James and Deidre walked along, trying to look like they were taking a stroll. Enough people were about the path enjoying the nice summer like weather. They stopped occasionally to appear to take in the beautiful day. But the men didn't stop.

In fact, the agents seemed to have sped up. They were going to lose them. Just then, the agents stopped and walked into the rows of cars parked in the field. She watched them head to a 1914 Packard. The village wasn't exactly a reflection of the more modern times, so an older car was not that unusual of a sight. But the exact year had to mean one thing. It was the time vehicle. It had to hold Max.

She had put her crystal back on, having fully charged it with James. She blushed thinking about last night. Her heart belonged to two men; it was clear now. But she longed to see Max again. She couldn't tell James how much Max meant to her. It had been so long since she had seen him. Everything she'd done this year was for this moment, to save him.

She got her focus back and remembered to check the sync on her bracelet with James's time vehicle. She knew she could remote control it as long as she was in range. She pushed the button now for it to come closer, parked just a few rows down from where the agents were. She walked near the cars, watching to see what they would do. One man opened the door and tossed the food in a bag to someone inside.

"Nice, boys. It's hard to eat with my hands tied." It was Max's voice.

"Well, I'm not going to feed ya."

"Come on, Hawkins, you can at least undo my hands. I can't run with my feet still tied."

The man leaned down and flicked out a pocketknife. He cut the bonds on Max's wrists. "There. Now shut up and eat."

Max leaned out of the car, rubbing his wrists. "That feels better. At least I can eat now." Deidre tried to breathe. He looked fine except for a bruised eye. He must have gotten it during his fight with them.

"I'm going to go around behind the vehicle," Deidre said to James. "Walk in front like you're still on a stroll. Try to get Max's attention." James started to move across the parking lot. She kept walking, knowing she had to look like the other people walking to their cars in the lot, but she kept an eye on the agents.

The other agent looked around. "Think I'll go scout around town and find us a place to stay tonight. It's going to be a while before we can make another jump. We should start with resting." He took out a gun and handed it to Hawkins. "Watch him. If he does anything, shoot him in the foot. That really hurts."

"Sure." Hawkins answered, then turned to Max. "This time we won't heal you up with the med kit."

Max tried to laugh with his mouth full. "Thanks. I get the idea. As it is, it's still tender."

"It only just grazed you. So stop whining. This time, I'll shoot to make it count." Hawkins pointed the gun at Max. "Hurry up and eat. I want you to be done by the time he comes back."

Deidre saw her chance. She hid behind one of the parked cars, listening for the other agent to leave. She watched through the car window as he walked toward the bridge. Inching behind the cars, she started making her move toward Agent Hawkins. She listened to their conversation, wondering how she was going to signal Max. She knew James would have made it to the other side by now. This might be it.

Hawkins stood with one foot resting on the running board of the car. "So, what made you do it, Max? Why did you save her?"

Max finished chewing his sandwich. "I'm in love with her."

"You put your career and the future of the Council on the line, because of love?"

"Yes. I gave up everything for love."

"Really. It can't be more important than the ability to time travel. If her kid lives, he'll vote down the research that helps put the wheels in motion for time travel. It's like stopping us before we even get started."

"That's the point. She is everything to me. And I figured I could intervene and stop it."

"Stop the pregnancy?"

At that point, Deidre eased up behind the car. She saw James on the other side. She stood just behind Hawkins with her finger over her lips. Max didn't miss a beat, but kept going. "Yes. In fact, I'm hoping that won't happen. If she gives everything for love too."

"And how could she do that?"

Deidre struck Hawkins in a neck with the butt of her gun, just as Max struck him from the front. Between both of their hits, the agent was knocked out cold. James rushed forward to find the agent unconscious on the ground.

"What took you so long?" Max smiled devilishly at Deidre and James.

"What? I've been waiting a whole year for you to show up. And that's all you can say to me?" She put her hands on her hips.

"No. But I'm so happy to see you both. Now, get me untied."

"Where's his pocketknife?"

"In his front suit pocket."

Deidre reached in and fished out the pocketknife. James pulled Hawkins' limp body away from the car door, so Deidre could cut the rope around Max's feet.

"Good to see you made it, Max." James placed his hand on his shoulder.

"Better late than never. See you took care of Deidre. Is the baby safe?"

Deidre stopped a moment. "What the hell are you talking about? How did you know about the baby?"

"James came up with it. He figured if I could get to you and cause a rift between you and the sculptor, it would begin the Resistance that had started to come up on the timeline. This is the start of everything, Deidre."

"Everything?" She looked between the both of them.

"Yes, the whole future of time travel changes with us." Max rubbed his hands together. "The power is going to shift now, and the Council will lose its grip over timeanauts. We'll become the real explorers we're meant to be. If we time it right, if you don't mind the pun."

"But we've got to get going now. There's only one more thing to do." Max looked at Deidre, and then back at James.

"What's that?" Deidre asked.

"Thank the both of you for saving me,." Max said.

James looked at Deidre and then back at Max. "She's waited an awful long time for you, mate." He winked at Max.

"I'm not a prize, gentlemen." Both men slowly looked at her.

Max spoke first. "Your anything but that. You're the love of my life that has just saved me." Max moved closer, wrapping his arms around her. "I want to show you how grateful I am."

"I've waited a long time for you to finally say that," She reached up to his face. "You're finally here."

"Yes I am." He stroked her cheek and kissed her. There was the unmistakable zing of metal hitting metal. Deidre turned her head to see the other agent running toward them, gun firing.

"Shit. Quick, everyone in the car." James grabbed the door handle, and jumped in. Max pulled Deidre in. Shots hit the outside as she reached and pulled the door closed. James took his crystal from his bracelet, and slid it into the energy slot. The rumble of the car threw them off balance as they started their getaway.

Max shouted. "Move out of town onto the main road."

"What speed?" The computer voice of the car asked.

"Twenty-five miles per hour." There was another ping as the bullet hit the outside. "Damn, he just doesn't give up."

James looked out behind them. "He's running fast." He started to wave through the window. "He's going to be in a pinch if this was the only vehicle they came in. It will be awhile before the Counsel can send another." He smiled wickedly. "I hope he likes 1928."

"No, the other agents were still on the lookout for Deidre. They were checking ahead of us in 1928."

"Good thing I jumped to 1927."

Max laughed. "That would explain why they weren't finding you in the timeline on that year. They were too busy thinking you'd follow procedure." He kissed her check. "That's my girl."

"So, why don't we still do a quick jump a few years ahead. It should outfox them for a little while. Then we can rendezvous with your son, Max."

"My son?"

Deidre blushed. "James put nanoparticles on the locket to counteract our NaNoBots. It turns them off for awhile. Kind of stuns our system until the nanoparticles wear off." She paused to meet his eyes. "My baby is yours."

"But I thought he was the sculptor's. That's how it read on the timeline."

"You changed it, mate." James leaned forward and hit him on the arm. "You're a father."

Max ran his fingers through his hair. "I never expected this."

"Father of the Time Rogues, really." Deidre wrapped her arm through his.

"That's not good, mate." James looked at Max's wrist.

"They must have discharged your energy in your bracelet so you wouldn't escape, right?."

Max held up his bracelet. His bracelet had no glow. "Yeah. Procedure they said. The agents drained the charge into the vehicle."

"It can't be left like that James. We're going to be on the run, and you need your bracelet charged in case either of us don't make it." James looked from one to the other. "We should be safe for a while. That means one thing." James looked at them both. "Max, you need to charge your bracelet now in case we have problems down the way."

Deidre looked from one man to the other. She swallowed. "Are you suggesting what I think?"

The movement of the car rocked her gently. James moved near to her on the other side of the leather seat. He grabbed her hand "Never been more serious. I do believe we are both madly in love with you. I can't think of anything better than to have both of us, together, show you how we feel. Am I right, Max?"

Max pulled Deidre toward him. She sank into his strong arms as his mouth leaned behind her ear. "I've been in love with you since training, Deidre. James has helped me get this far. We've been in this together to save you. If it wasn't for him, neither of us would have you now." He caressed her neck and down her breasts. "For that, I'm thankful to him."

The swaying of the car rocked her gently as Max and James started to remove her clothes. Max pulled her skirt down while James undid the buttons of her blouse. She closed her eyes, letting her arms drop to her sides as the men undressed her. She felt lips leaning over her, brushing against her forehead. Then, finding her lips. Kissing them so deeply her toes curled.

She felt her shoes and stockings being pulled off, and opened her eyes to see Max leaning over her silky knickers, pulling the edges to expose her wetness that was building between her legs. The two men she loved were with her now.

She opened her legs as Max removed his work shirt, unbuttoning the front, and pulling it off his shoulders. She felt James moving behind her to remove his clothes. She reached behind to feel his hard chest. There was an intake of his breath as her fingers caressed him. She smiled. "I can't make a choice between you. I love you both.."

James whispered, emotion choking his voice. "You don't have to, Deidre. We're both here."

She reached for him. He moved his face over her whispering, "We chose you.."

James's lips brushed her again as Max moved over her, leaning over her body. She felt James move back to hold her, wrapping his arms around her, pulling her against his chest, supporting her.. His hands explored her naked torso as Max moved over the top of her, kissing her neck, down the center of her breasts, and over her stomach. Max reached down between her legs, feeling the moisture that begged him to take her. "This is for everything that we've been through, Deidre."

Max leaned over her. Deidre felt James caressing her from behind. His touch sent sensual chills down her torso as he stroked up to her breasts, rubbing the nipples into peaks. Max moved to part her thighs, rubbing his fingers over her nub, pushing in the spot to send a shudder through her. James held her tighter. Goosebumps went up on her arms where the hairs of James's arms met hers.

Max moved his hands along her hips and she opened her legs, ready for him. "Deidre, you are my everything." Max's whisper was punctuated by the thrust from his entry. James's arms grabbed her tighter, kissing her neck. She gave herself over to the men loving her. All thought left her as Max thrust in her again and again. James's lips sent waves of lust through her in electric sparks. She felt the climax build to its peak and release through her body in wave after wave of rapture.

She let herself lean into James, and reached out for Max. She closed her eyes and whispered,. "I'm lucky to have you both. I love the both of you."

"We're lucky to still have you, Deidre." She felt James's chest rumble with his words.

"We gave everything up for your love," Max answered beside her.

She settled against James, and squeezed Max's lean form lying next to her. "We have each other now. All through time."

About the Author

Marilyn Vix writes fast-paced paranormal romances with strong females finding their HEA with hot warlocks, vampires, and time travelers. She currently lives in Northern California with her husband. This is her first full-length novel.

Marilyn is currently working on her first full-length contemporary romance, *Saving My Heart* and the second book in the Time Rogue series. She has a novella paranormal romance series called Beware of Warlocks with the first book entitled, *Never Marry A Warlock*. For more information about her books, visit her website at:

MARILYNVIX.COM

Acknowledgments

Every writing project is an adventure. I'd like to thank those that have brought me to this point in my journey. To my husband, you are my human cat. Thank you for making me purr when I need it the most. To my beta reader that give it to me straight, Alain Gomez, thank you. To my editor Shelley Holloway, thank you for the polish you give all of my work. You make it all shiny. Your encouragement keeps me going and in the panic moments, "Don't worry, it's fixable" can limit my meltdowns.

Thank you to Robin J. Samuels of Shadowcat Editing for getting the manuscript combed and polished. You put in the final touches on a three year project. Its perfection makes me finally be able to breath, it's finally done, and I didn't have to worry when I handed my baby over for its final prep.

Most of all, I'd like to thank my readers. Thank you for all the encouragement during the Kindle Scout campaign. Even though it wasn't picked, I know that you all wanted it. It is now living and breathing because of your support. To have you all enjoy my books makes it all worthwhile. Thank you to all my readers for being a part of my writing journey.

Be sure to check out my website for more information and sign up for my newsletter. I'll be feverish working on the next book in the series. All updates can be found there.

One last request, if you enjoyed this book, please consider leaving a review on Goodreads.com or Amazon.com. Reviews really do help let other readers know your opinions and help people find it. I also would really appreciate hearing your thoughts. I often consider them while writing the next book. So, I hope to read your review soon.

Other books by Marilyn Vix:

Never Marry A Warlock Omnibus Edition

www.amazon.com/Never-Marry-Warlock-Omnibus-Marilyn-ebook/dp/B01EQGUTOA

For the latest information about new releases, promos, or just tell me how you felt about this novel, visit my website at:

MARILYNVIX.COM.

Newsletter Link: eepurl.com/MWT2L

Find Marilyn Vix on social media at:
Facebook: https://www.facebook.com/marilyn.vix
Twitter: https://twitter.com/MarilynVix
Pinterest: https://www.pinterest.com/marilynvix/

38383545R00157

Made in the USA
Columbia, SC
05 December 2018